This book is dedicated to my beloved husband

Harold Arthur Bennett

The Funeral Singer

Anhua Gao

Remembering Publishing LLC

The Funeral Singer

Anhua Gao

ISBN: 978-1-68560-068-6 (Print)
          978-1-68560-069-3 (eBook)

LCCN: 2023 907264

May 2023, First Edition, First Printing

Remembering Publishing, LLC
RememPub@gmail.com

INTRODUCTION

We Chinese believe that death has no favourites. When we die it matters not how rich or famous our parents, or how much or how little that we ourselves have achieved. The only importance is how we treated other living things during our time on earth. Our only birthright is death, and when it comes, every spirit is equally and fairly judged.

However, because those left behind insist on giving the recently departed a good send-off, or as we Chinese say, "on the road" or "down the road", the same cannot be said about funeral ceremonies. Snobbishness, social status, superstition and local custom are just a few of the factors that make the disposal of our remains a complicated business.

Although ceremonies surrounding body disposal vary, funerals everywhere have things in common - much weeping, funereal music, songs and sad faces. That's where the professionals enter the picture. They ease the pain of bereavement by making sure that the dead are publicly honoured and respectfully disposed of.

*

Despite sixty years of Communist suppression, superstition still exercises a powerful influence in China. In many areas outside the cities and larger towns, no amount of political interference has managed to completely stop people from following their ancient rites and rules of ceremony. In some of our remote villages, wooden horns and brass bugles are blown and drums are loudly beaten at funerals to chase away the evil spirits. Such things ensure that the recently departed has a good journey down the road to the next world. Which, to us Chinese, is under the ground.

When we talk to the dead we don't raise our eyes to the sky. We drop onto all fours and kow-tow with our foreheads almost touching the ground. We call on our ancestors at special times like, for example, marriage. During a traditional marriage ceremony, the bride and groom bow to their ancestors and ask them to approve the union by sending healthy children.

Our funeral ceremonies include leaving food for eating and the burning of imitation money for the spirit to use in the next world. Every April, during the Sweeping Tomb Festival, the family will gather at the burial ground to give the graves of their ancestors a spring clean, leave more food and burn more imitation paper money.

Sometimes firecrackers are set off. Not to mourn a loved one but to celebrate the death of a bad person, turning a funeral into a happy event. Ancient writings teach us that Yama is the King of the Nether World. He keeps a record of everything each of us has done whilst alive and every new underground arrival is assigned a level according to the way he or she lived their earthly life. Layer one for the best behaved, layer two for the next best and so on down the layers to our version of Hell.

Called Di-Yu, meaning Underground Prison, our Hell is on level eighteen - the lowest level. It is believed that the noise of the firecrackers will chase the spirit of the hated one deep under the ground to Di-Yu where he or she will be repeatedly boiled in oil for all eternity.

Yama is also the controller of birth and death. He decides who is to die and when. He also chooses what spirit will replace them. During his rounds of the Nether World, Yama will suddenly kick a spirit back to the earth and into a womb at the exact moment the woman conceives. This explains why many newborn babies have a bruise on their backside.

*

Our community has grown from one hut some three thousand years ago into three individual villages that, together, can be called a town. During the early years there was only one family name, so everyone was given a nickname. Today the majority of the inhabitants still have nicknames because, after centuries of closed-in life, they still share only a dozen or so family names.

One example of that is the local funeral singer. His name is Han Lao-lao. There are lots of people living in the three villages with the family name of Han so his nickname, for reasons you will quickly understand, is La-la.

*

Situated in the northwest corner of China, our three villages nestle in a valley between three mountains. It is remote, quiet and extraordinarily peaceful. The summers are gentle and warm causing few deaths, but when the fierce cold of winter comes and the snows fall, the number of funerals in our region are at their highest. It is also the time when sudden loud sounds can easily bring down avalanches so during the winter months we need quiet ceremonies. No loud wailing, no horns or bugles and definitely no firecrackers.

By Chinese peasant standards, we who live in the valley are lucky. The land is rich and fertile and throughout the centuries, most of the many wars that have ravaged China have passed us by. Rulers have come and gone without changing our traditional ways. Then, in 1949, the Communists defeated the Nationalists and took power in China, bringing a completely new way of life.

Like other remote areas of China, there is almost no schooling, so few of us can read or write. The Communists are now our masters. If we need help with anything, we must turn to the local Communist leaders for their advice and guidance. We must also obey their orders.

Some things have been slow to change. For example, to our superstitious population, the slightest involvement in the handling of a dead member of another family will bring bad luck, making death a family affair. Whilst poor families do almost everything themselves, richer families employ poor peasants to do it for them. When the belly is empty, money usually overrides superstition.

As death has always been a frequent visitor due to our hard peasant life, the family elders are well versed in the ancient writings on the correct way to wash, dress and lay out the dead and how to organise a funeral. Nevertheless, before burial was outlawed in favour of cremation, one professional built up such a high reputation; his participation became an obligatory part of every funeral. He was La-la, The Funeral Singer, and if he was not involved in a funeral, the deceased family lost much face.

(When we say "face" we mean good name and approbation.)

*

For a thousand years our local singer of songs has been a same-family business, passing from father to son down to La-la. Traditionally the singer of songs is the first person to be called out after a death.

With La-la, the people were extraordinarily lucky. From the age of twelve when his father began to teach him, he loved his job of singing wonderful songs sung beautifully. And despite the busy periods leaving him no time for himself, he never let anyone down.

Educationally illiterate, he inherited a wonderful voice and a gift for poetry, which he coupled with beautiful melodies composed entirely from his own imagination. His songs are known as "on the road ballads" and he never sang a song more than once, making every funeral as individual as the life just ended.

Except for a pair of twinkling, extremely kind eyes, physically he was not good to look at. His short squat body, spiky hair, overhanging brow and bulbous nose hid a sweet nature and a loving disposition. But it is his voice that is forever remembered. Gentle and melodious, it never failed to touch the hearts of the living like a soft breeze floating through their emotions.

In the days before Communism, La-la used to lead the processions towards the grave. And a legend says that at many funerals led by La-la, mourners witnessed the recently departed walking alongside the body and upon arrival at the graveside, to smilingly disappear into the earth, leaving life behind.

For all of his working life La-la enjoyed the enviable position of knowing that every family would need him at some time, and yet, whilst everybody knew how important his job was, nobody wanted it.

This is his story, told with love and respect.

TABLE OF CONTENTS

CHAPTER 1

Yellow Station

One evening in June 1985 Comrade Woo Song helped his family alight from a train stopped at Yellow Station. He hadn't chosen to bring them to this remote part of China but felt fortunate that they had arrived safely. He also considered himself twice lucky to have held on to his position as a low-grade cadre within the Chinese Communist Party. What's more, despite not being guilty of any crime, he and his family had been forced to flee the city and return to the place of his conception.

Where once there had only been footpaths criss-crossing the mountains, Yellow Station sits alongside a single-track railway line that runs through the valleys and mountains between Beijing and Xi'an, a distance of some one thousand kilometres. Although the line is not busy it is a fast link for the people living in this remote area to the outside world, making it important to them.

Every day four trains run one way and four the other. While most are express trains dashing importantly between the two major cities, slow trains chug along carrying peasants and local dignitaries to and from the remote farming communes and their nearest towns. Whenever an express train is due, the local train has to reverse into a siding and wait until its speedy cousin, belching out smoke and steam, whooshes past and disappears into the next tunnel.

This line runs through a sparsely populated region and is possibly the most boring and uninteresting train journey in China. For most of their time on the train, passengers have nothing to look at except grey mountain granite rising up on both sides of the track. Or nothing at all when they are carried through numerous seemingly endless black tunnels. However there is one short section of the line that seasoned passengers look forward to passing through, and experience a feeling of wellbeing every time they do.

*

Early in the 20th century, when the Last Emperor was still on the throne, the local Mandarin, an influential member of the nearby City Council, named his vast estate "Commissioner Ding Gang's County" after himself. He was a pompous man full of his own importance. His father had not supported the laying of the rail track through his land but Ding Gang liked the idea of having his own station. And anyway, the Empress Dowager had approved the project, making all objections inapplicable.

By the time the line was ready for use the Qing Dynasty had died and so had the old man, giving the son a free hand. He had a railway station built in a five hundred-metre length of open-air track between two long tunnels. And because yellow was his favorite colour everything on the station had to be yellow. Yellow buildings, yellow platform and yellow uniformed staff.

During the inaugural opening ceremony the station was given the name, Commissioner Ding Gang's Personal Station. He was not a particularly popular man to cause his name to be remembered so it wasn't long after his funeral that the station name was changed by local usage to Yellow Station, and the Mandarin's estate became known as Yellow County.

The local people have always felt pride in their station. It has survived many political upheavals such as the Japanese occupation of China followed by a brutal civil war between the Nationalists and the Communists. The Communists won and took power in China in October 1949.

In 1966, at the beginning of Mao Zedong's Cultural Revolution, the people successfully resisted demands from Red Guard extremists to dispatch the Stationmaster, his Deputy and the porters for "re-education" in the paddy fields.

The Red Guards also wanted to repaint the station a blood red colour and change the area name to Red County.

"Red is for socialism, yellow is decadent and morally corrupt," said the Red Guards.

"Nonsense!" Countered the people. "Yellow is the colour of the five stars on our revolutionary flag."

The Red Guards had no answer to that so people power won the day. The station staff stayed in place, the station stayed yellow and the area continued to be called Yellow County. That's how Yellow Station continued to be a bright spring-like oasis amid dull granite and dark tunnels.

The station routine has not changed much. Every morning at exactly ten minutes to eight o'clock the Stationmaster, his Deputy and all five porters step out of their respective living quarters onto the platform to form a line facing the railway track to greet the first train of the day.

And since that first morning in 1915 when the Stationmaster ushered the proud Mandarin into his special compartment on the morning train to town, five smiling porters have waved it away into the tunnel.

Following the death of the Mandarin the routine changed slightly. Whilst the Stationmaster stands to attention overseeing all activities, the porters help passengers with their luggage and the Deputy, a brightly polished silver whistle swinging from a yellow ribbon around his neck, holds a small green flag in his right hand and a red flag in his left. It is his job to stop the train at exactly the right place by waving the red flag, see that all passengers are clear and all doors are closed before blowing a short blast on the whistle. If all is well he will then wave the green flag.

This is the signal to the driver to get the train moving. By that time the porters have lined up to wave the train away.

Non-stop express trains are not ignored. The Deputy and the porters happily wave them through and the passengers love it. After so much blackness and granite, the bright and clean yellow station with the immaculately turned out yellow uniformed staff enthusiastically waving and smiling is a uniquely happy experience.

*

The layout of the station is not special. Along the full length of the yellow painted concrete platform, single-storey wooden buildings have been built. There is a ticket office, waiting room, left luggage store and a tool-shed. The porters live at the south end of the platform in a wooden structure similar to an army hut. It contains five single beds, each with a bedside locker and a wardrobe. There is a dining table ringed by five chairs and a huge leather sofa - a gift from a grateful passenger. Dominating the centre of the hut is a smoky wood-burning stove used for warmth, hot water and cooking. A door at the rear leads to a small room where the porters wash themselves and their clothes in a large tin sink. All water is drawn from a well and must be boiled before use.

The Deputy has a separate two-roomed flatlet at the north end. Only Stationmaster has a house. The ground floor consists of a living room, dining room, office and kitchen. There are three bedrooms upstairs. His house is set apart, behind the station. The position of Stationmaster is considered important enough for him to be allocated funds to employ a cook and a cleaner. The Deputy and the porters fend for themselves.

To the rear of the station there are three holes dug in the ground, one behind the other, with each hole surrounded by its own wicker fence. They are the toilets. The front hole is for the exclusive use of the Stationmaster. The second is for the Deputy and the third is for the porters.

Yellow Station has never been busy. In remote areas most people spend their waking hours working the land simply to stay alive. Few have the time or the money to ride the trains. Daily, only two trains stop. Eight o'clock in the morning going to town and five-fifteen in the evening coming back. Nevertheless there is plenty to occupy the staff. As soon as the eight o'clock train disappears into the tunnel, the Deputy and four of the porters change into yellow overalls and begin cleaning, mending, painting or working on the smallholding. The staff grow most of their own vegetables and keep chickens, rabbits, pigs and goats. The fifth porter is on duty for that day. He takes care of any ticket sales, left luggage, mail and parcel movements. The duty porter has little to do, making it a nice rest day in an otherwise busy work schedule.

All through the day, whenever an express is due, the staff wash and change back into their smart yellow uniforms to line up along the platform. The Stationmaster salutes, the Deputy stands to attention and the porters wave and smile at the running train. In return the passengers wave and smile and the engine driver lets out two short loud whistles. The only change to this routine is when the winter snows arrive. For fear of starting an avalanche the train whistle stays silent.

And so it has always been.

*

In 1950, not long after the Communists took power, the descendants of the long dead Mandarin were slaughtered and their house commandeered for use as the office and residence of the local Communist leader. Whilst leaders have come and gone the house continues to be the local seat of power.

At the same time as the first Communist leader took over the county, the station staff were replaced by members of the Communist Party. The new men did not ask for the job, the Party assigned them. Fortunately the new county leader, mindful of local pride, had insisted that the old staff remain long enough to teach the new men the old traditions.

And so it goes. Not much happens to disturb the endless rotation of duty, trains and work. Once a year the leader of Yellow County Town Railway Bureau visits for two hours. His special train rolls up, he alights and consumes a sumptuous lunch whilst his secretary checks the official ledgers. With the inspection over for another year, the leader burps his way back onto his train and departs.

For several years the station staff remained single and did their glorious work (as described by the Party) without complaint. They had arrived as young men full of ideas about wife and family but no woman wanted to live in such a remote place. Any woman that showed an interest was quickly deterred by the thought of maybe having seven males to care for.

The seven men had their annual two-week holidays in turn. During these holidays they returned to their home villages or towns hoping to find a wife. Year after year all failed until, in 1959, Woo Bao, the Deputy, got lucky. Through a marriage-broker he successfully met Li Lan, a woman from a poor place where people did not have enough to eat.

At their first meeting she took one look at the yellow uniform and decided that Comrade Woo Bao must be a rich and important Party official. Without hesitation she agreed to the marriage thinking that a long and easy life stretched away in front of her. And she was very impressed to learn that her husband had unlimited free travel on the railways of China and as his wife she would enjoy the same privilege! So, after the official marriage formalities had been taken care of she happily allowed her new husband to whisk her away to Yellow Station before she changed her mind.

In the eyes of the bachelors, Li Lan was a bright star. All offered help to make her life as pleasant as possible. That first night she invited everyone to dinner in her new home. When serving up the dishes she commented, "With a proper kitchen I could cook much better meals."

The next day the men began to build a kitchen next to the living room. When they had finished Li Lan surveyed their work. The yellow-painted kitchen had a wood-burning stove with a chimney going out through a side wall. It had working surfaces, a new wok and lots of pots, pans, dishes, cups and chopsticks. She was mightily satisfied and settled down to domestic life on Yellow Station.

Her man, as the Deputy Stationmaster, did not have to work in the smallholding or do any maintenance. He toured the platform checking for wear and tear and signs of inefficiency and sometimes he walked along the track knocking here and there with a hammer whilst she leaned on the door of her home and looked at him.

Being a wife was easy, exactly as she had always dreamed it would be. Then two things happened. Winter came early with a sudden blast of freezing wind followed by a blizzard - and she was pregnant.

It was horrendously cold. The men were used to such conditions but not Li Lan. She was from the warmth of the plains. When her comfortable world suddenly changed she couldn't cope. Even worse she craved the taste of sour plums but couldn't have any. Then it was an urgent yearning for young green apples.

With the area completely snowed in and living with a husband who couldn't satisfy her pregnant cravings, Li Lan felt let down. Her life felt empty - as dry as parched earth and her miserable face showed her unhappiness. Woo Bao tried everything to get his wife to smile but misery was her constant companion. Every evening Woo Bao fetched bucket after bucket of water from the well and chopped wood for the stove. He boiled the water and prepared a tub for Li Lan to wash her body. Before she retired for the night Woo Bao gave her a massage and tucked her up in the big bed whilst he slept on the floor. It didn't help. Li Lan had made up her mind to be miserable and nothing was going to stop her... except a proper bathroom.

"City people go to a proper communal bathroom and I used to go too before I married you," she wailed. "It was very good. You are an official. Why can't you build me a bathroom?"

The first time Woo Bao heard this, it came as a complete surprise. He knew that his wife had come from a poor village where the village pond was the only source of water, and a good wash - meaning a splash of pond water over hands and face, happened only once or twice a year. Now she was demanding a *Bathroom!* Who did she think she was? An Empress?

He gave it some thought. His beautiful Li Lan deserved to be given her heart's desire at this critical time but it wouldn't be easy. No sensible man would begin a building project in the middle of winter and anyway, it was impossible to get the necessary materials delivered until the spring. But none of that mattered. If his wife wanted a bathroom, then he should build one. Wasn't she worth it? Of course she was! He had spent years looking for a wife. Now that she was here he must do everything to make her happy.

That is why a few days later, despite the fact that the baby was not due for several months, he reluctantly agreed when Li Lan told him that she wanted to take a trip into town. She could have a proper bath, eat some of her favourite nibbles and buy some baby things ready for the birth. Meanwhile, he thought, he would begin building a bathroom as her homecoming surprise.

By now the track had been cleared and the trains were running. When Woo Bao gently escorted Li Lan to her seat, she had his entire salary for one year, some 500 yuan, sewn into her clothing.

"Take this money and have a wonderful time," he had said. "It will take us half-a-month to build a bathroom, so I will expect you back in fifteen days or so. When you see the yellow buildings you will be safely back home."

Woo Bao and the porters worked hard. It was bitterly cold but they persevered until a small yellow-painted wooden house stood alongside the left luggage store. Above the door a sign read, "Bathroom For Ladies Only." Passengers coming and going read the words and wondered why a ladies-only bathroom had been built. Was there also going to be a bathroom for the men? Apparently not. How strange!

*

Not only did Li Lan not return, she went even further away to the big city of Xi'an. With 500 yuan on offer, despite being pregnant she easily found a city man willing to marry her before she gave birth to a son and named him Woo Song. Her ambition was for him to grow and become a real city official, or a People's Servant, as the Party called them. And twenty-five years later, in 1985, that is exactly what happened.

Woo Song, already happily married with a two-year-old daughter and a member of the Communist Party, was promoted to the lowest grade of cadre and sent to work in the Cultural Affairs Bureau of the local People's Government. It was happy moment. With his career on the rise and his wife, Shu Mei, supervising the busy video, music cassettes and compact discs section of a local department store, their future looked very good indeed. Then a new Chinese-made movie called "Red Sorghum" was shown in the local cinema.

Woo Song and Shu Mei wanted very much to see the film but the cinema tickets at 30 yuan per person were expensive. Their budget meant making a choice between seeing the film or buying new clothes for their daughter.

They did not go to the cinema.

Shu Mei said to her husband, "Never mind. Video Compact Disc, or VCD's as they are called, has arrived at our shop. It's a new recording concept of listening and seeing pictures on the television at the same time. When the Red Sorghum discs arrive I can borrow the VCD player used for demonstrating the system and buy the discs at staff discount."

Two weeks later the film, recorded onto two discs, was delivered to the store. After getting permission to take the VCD player home for one night, Shu Mei purchased the two discs at the special price of 5 yuan.

That evening after dinner, whilst Shu Mei connected the VCD player to the television, Song washed his child and coaxed her to bed earlier than usual. Then he and Shu Mei settled down to watch the film.

As the first coloured images flashed onto the television screen, Song was impressed and excited to see this new concept in home entertainment. Suddenly something went wrong. A mosaic of small multicoloured squares replaced the picture.

"Damn it," cursed Shu Mei. "It's a faulty disc."

"Everything is faulty these days," said Song. "What can you expect for 5 yuan?"

To which remark the disappointed Shu Mei angrily answered, "I'm going to contact the supplier and get a replacement. I won't be cheated so easily!"

So, although the next day was Shu Mei's day off, she left home at her usual time, leaving her daughter in the care of Li Lan, now a widow. Shu Mei's first priority was to return the VCD player to her workplace before going to the supplier to ask for the discs to be changed or her money back.

She was offered replacement discs but not a refund.

All right, said she, provided that she could check that the replacement discs were acceptable. Unfortunately she couldn't find one good disc. Nor could she get her money back.

"Once the goods are sold, it is the buyers' responsibility," said the supplier.

Anger rose up in Shu Mei. "You are a thief and a cheat," she shouted at the man. "Never before have I heard such rubbish. You must be punished and I intend to see that you get what you deserve."

She went to her husband.

*

Everywhere in China, those working in the Cultural Affairs Bureau are in charge of retail sales including the audio and visual home entertainment market. Checking for faulty goods is part of their job - a job with rich pickings. When checking the shops, the People's Servants are wined, dined and given red envelopes full of cash to say nothing about any inferior goods they might find.

Everyone takes his or her cut of the bribes. The biggest share goes to Beijing; the smallest to the lowest grade of cadre like Woo Song. This is the way business is done in China.

When Shu Mei stormed into his office, Song immediately knew what was wrong. She had failed to get satisfaction over the discs. Although new to the Bureau he had heard about the bribery system and intended to take full advantage of it. He cursed himself for not thinking to telephone the supplier and telling him to make Shu Mei happy. Now here she was bent on revenge.

He listened to her tirade until he could take no more. He was losing much face. Through the glass partition he could see his smirking colleagues gathered in the corridor. He couldn't just sit there so he took the only option open to him.

"Come with me," he said to his wife. "I will introduce you to my boss, Comrade Director Feng. You can tell him."

Director Feng gave a sympathetic hearing to Shu Mei. In front of her husband's boss Shu Mei spoke quietly and explained everything clearly. Nevertheless there was no doubting her outrage at the way she had been treated. When she had finished her tale the Director showed the correct amount of anger.

"How dare this man bully the wife of one of my men! Leave this matter with me. I will see that you get justice."

A mollified Shu Mei returned home. When he was alone the Director made a few telephone calls.

Later that day three bureau staff members paid a visit to the supplier and closed him down. When they returned to the office Song was given 10 yuan and shown a plastic sack full of confiscated discs. One man said, "You can tell your wife that she has been avenged."

A relieved Woo Song and a satisfied Shu Mei slept soundly that night unaware of the danger they were in. They had disturbed a nest of vipers. At their head was a ruthless gangster known as a Snakehead. He in turn was protected by a high-ranking government official, making the organisation very powerful and above the law.

*

A few days later Song was sitting at his desk sifting through a pile of mundane paperwork when Director Feng knocked politely and entered. Song jumped to his feet but was waved down by his boss. The Director also sat.

Taking out his cigarettes he offered one to Song.

Director Feng asked, "How do you like your job Comrade Woo?"

"I like it fine thank you Comrade Director."

"I have heard good things about you. And how is your wife? Has she recovered from that unpleasant experience?"

"Yes, Comrade Director. She is quite happy now that she has her money back. Thanks to you the matter is now settled."

"Good," said Feng. "Then she won't make a fuss if the supplier, Master Ling, is allowed to re-open his business?"

"I'm sorry Comrade Director, I don't quite under…"

Feng interrupted. "Master Ling has paid me a visit. He agrees that the Red Sorghum discs were faulty but claims that he is entirely blameless. He contacted the company that presses the discs and they stopped production to check output and discovered a problem. Apparently, because of the huge demand for the Red Sorghum discs, nobody stopped to check the quality. He says your wife was the first to complain and thought that she must have been mistaken until other faulty discs were discovered. Although not at fault he takes full responsibility for the incident. I told him that you were handling this case and he must talk to you. You can decide how best to settle the matter."

Feng rose, stubbed out his cigarette, winked conspiratorially and ended with, "I'll send him along."

A few minutes later Master Ling sidled into Song's office. Smiling broadly but uneasily and repeatedly bowing, he introduced himself before saying, "Comrade Woo. Please forgive me. This misunderstanding is all my doing. I have brought you the discs your wife wanted and I guarantee to supply all your future needs free of charge."

This was the moment when Song endangered the lives of himself and his family. He was young and inexperienced with a young man's arrogance. He did not take the discs. Instead he put on an air of superiority.

"Can't you see that I am busy?" he snapped. "I have no time or desire to discuss this matter at the moment."

He returned his attention to the pile of papers on his desk, making it clear that the meeting was adjourned. He didn't look up. That is why he didn't see the look of pure poison that crossed Master Ling's face as he bowed himself out of the office.

For the remainder of that day Song felt good about himself. He was sure that his boss would be impressed with the way he had handled the matter. Director Feng was not in his office when Song dropped off his written report on his meeting with Master Ling.

It was after dark when Song left his office and made his way out of the building. As he was descending the concrete steps to the street a smiling Master Ling called, "Comrade Woo, please allow me to speak."

Song's silence was confirmation enough to Master Ling that he could continue.

"I was wrong. I never should have treated your wife so badly. Please allow me to make amends. I have sent the discs by courier to your home together with my personal note of apology and now I invite you to dinner in the best restaurant in town."

Song hesitated. He was very flattered. He had never been able to afford to eat in the first, the second, or even the third best eating-place in town. Apart from home, his meals were purchased from cheap pavement food vendors.

Master Ling asked him again. "Please Comrade Woo. It is the least I can do."

Ten minutes later the two men were sitting at a table in a private room of the very best restaurant in town. Meanwhile back in the Cultural Affairs Building Director Feng, basically a decent man, was worried. "Woo Song and his wife are a well-intentioned young couple," he thought. "It is a pity. I would like to help but..." He shrugged. There wasn't much that he could do but given the chance, he knew that he would.

In the restaurant, Song's tongue wasn't working. It felt swollen and numb.

"From ... now on ... we are ... friends. We ... we ..." He passed out.

A few hours later a sharp sound jolted him awake. He was in unfamiliar surroundings, lying naked on a strange bed with a never-before-experienced morning-after hangover. What was even worse, beside him lay a young, naked, barely pubescent girl. A second bang demanded his attention. Beside the bed stood two policemen scowling down at him. One banged the bed-head a third time with his truncheon and shouted, "You filthy bastard! Put on your clothes and come with us."

*

His disgrace was absolute. The local newspaper printed an extremely salacious, largely untrue account of his misdeeds and the radio completed the job. Everybody now knew that he visited prostitutes and his personal preference was for prepubescent girls.

Whoring was a crime, especially for an official. All People's Servants were expected to be honourable and law-abiding; at least as far as the public were concerned. The girl was reported to be a child, making the case more serious. He was locked up to await investigation and trial.

According to the police they had acted upon an anonymous telephone tip-off giving the hotel and the room number. Song could offer no defence. His account of the incident was confused and incoherent. Luckily for him the police knew the girl as a young but already hardened professional. She knew that at worst she would be fined and released so it didn't hurt her to tell the truth. Her clear and calmly spoken version of the incident saved Song from a long prison sentence.

She said that a man she later identified as Master Ling paid her to have sex with Woo Song but he was already unconscious when he was carried to the bed so nothing happened. This bore out Woo Song's story. His last memory of that night was of being in the restaurant until being awakened by the police. He did not know how he had got to the bed nor had he any recollection of the girl. When he was accused of having sex with a child prostitute he couldn't believe it of himself. With visions of lost wife, daughter and job, "never" was his response. "Never... never... never!"

The police telephoned Director Feng who declared that there must be something more to the story. Comrade Woo was happily married with a young daughter.

"This case must be thoroughly investigated," he said. "Only compelling evidence will make me believe he is guilty."

That was the best that Director Feng could do for his young subordinate but it was enough. The police concluded that Master Ling, a non-Party member, had made a badly planned attempt to discredit Woo Song, a Party Cadre. Master Ling was arrested, tried and sentenced to five years hard labour.

In the same court Song was found guilty of being drunk in a public place and let off with a warning. If he was ever again caught drunk or with a prostitute, his punishment would be a hefty fine, expulsion from the Party, and a term of imprisonment.

A highly relieved but contrite Woo Song was released but the story did not die - local mean-mouths made sure of that. For weeks he had to endure gossip and see people pointing. In the office one particularly nasty woman took daily pleasure in making him the butt of her jokes by adding inflammatory details to the already juicy tale. He could not retort - she was a higher-grade cadre than he. His normally happy and pleasant disposition steadily disappeared to be replaced by surliness and bad temper.

At home, despite the police report, his wife continued to be suspicious of his every move. Trust had been damaged and his bad attitude made things worse.

At last he broke.

"All because of your bloody faulty discs," he shouted. "You started this fucking shambles. Piss off and leave me alone. If you want a divorce, get one. I don't care anymore."

At work, in an attempt to bring things back to normal, Director Feng convened a staff meeting. When everyone was present, Director Feng strode in and wasted no time on pleasantries.

"Comrades, I have waited, hoping that the malicious gossip about Comrade Woo Song would die down, but it hasn't. There are some in the Bureau who want to keep it going. So I say it stops right now. Understood?"

He glared around the room daring anyone to smile or giggle. Nobody did.

He continued, "Comrade Woo Song. Do you want to take this opportunity to explain yourself and to do your self-criticism?"

He looked encouragingly at his blushing subordinate. Woo Song moved to the front of the room, faced his colleagues and told them everything, leaving nothing out. Then he apologised for bringing shame upon the Bureau. He was naïve, he said. New to the job. Had a lot to learn. "I thought I knew my way around but I was wrong. I am a very stupid man and lucky to be here. I could be doing hard labour. Only Master Ling's bad planning, the truthfulness of a prostitute and help from Director Feng saved me." He turned towards Director Feng to say, "Thank you Comrade Director from the bottom of my heart."

To applause, he returned to his seat.

Director Feng ended the meeting with the news that Master Ling was dead. Whilst working in a quarry, falling rocks had killed him. As the staff filed out he asked Song to remain. When they were alone the cigarettes were produced and the two men settled for a chat.

The Director began with the thought that the meeting had gone well and the gossips had been silenced.

"There are some nasty people in this world," he lectured, "and those who enjoy spreading spiteful gossip are among the worst because they make sure that their victim cannot fight back. I hate them."

Song nodded and again thanked his boss. "I didn't know such things could happen," he said. "But a good thing has come from this. I have learned that I have a lot to learn."

Director Feng nodded and said sadly, "There is worse to come. The official verdict on the death of Master Ling is accident. It wasn't. He was murdered. If you had been convicted it would have been you."

A shocked Song stared at his boss and stammered, "I... I don't understand Comrade Director. Why kill Master Ling? Why kill me? And who did it?"

"Young man you must be constantly vigilant. There are dangerous forces at work in this country. Never drop your guard and trust nobody you don't know. Master Ling made a mess of framing you and paid the price. You are still free so I must conclude that you are in imminent danger. So are your wife and child. The people involved are mean and vicious. They enjoy killing. They have no mercy and they never forget. That is the truth and because I fear for you and your family, I want to help. Our first priority is to get you out of the city."

*

Song wasn't sure what he would find at home. His last words to his wife had been harsh. He stepped through the front door of their second floor one-bedroomed flat into Shu Mei's order and peace. He stopped for a moment to listen. Nothing. His wife and child were not at home. Walking into the living room he stood and looked around him. On an almost non-existent budget Shu Mei had turned the bare flat into a real home.

There was the strange-shaped black ornament she had brought home from the market. "Look," she had exclaimed, placing it on the windowsill. "It only cost three yuan and it looks perfect."

She had stood back to let him see her latest purchase and he remembered how her head had tilted at a slight angle. She had looked so beautiful that his breath had caught in his throat. Only now did he realise that the black of the ornament did look good against the white of the wall and he knew, just as he had always known from his first childhood memory. He loved Shu Mei with all of his heart.

He heard footsteps and girlish giggles. With a pounding heart he watched the door open and his wife and child enter. His daughter, Little Jasmine, ran to him and wrapped her short arms around his left leg and, to his great surprise and even greater relief, Shu Mei gave him a big smile. He picked up Little Jasmine and walked into the open arms of his wife.

That night, with Little Jasmine sleeping peacefully in her crib beside their bed, Song and Shu Mei quietly bonded, parted, and bonded again. Neither could sleep. They whispered their worries and their fears. Shu Mei now fully understood the turmoil she had caused. After the staff meeting, with Song out on an errand, Director Feng had spent two hours explaining the situation to Shu Mei and Song's mother, Li Lan. By the time the Director had finished they knew the whole story from Shu Mei's first visit to the Bureau to Song's self-criticism and the death of Master Ling. They understood how easily it had been for Song to be sucked into something that he was unable to control and that the whole family was in great danger. It was time to take protective action, but what?

Director Feng had promised to work on the problem and would let them know when he had something concrete. "However," he warned. "I have to get you out of the city. That means the remote countryside. The four of you will be alive and out of harm's way but you won't be going forward to a better life, more like backwards into hardship. What you make of it will be up to you."

Li Lan remembered Yellow Station. "Comrade Director, I have a suggestion.

CHAPTER 2

Cocky

In 1967, about a year after Chairman Mao had launched his Cultural Revolution, a medium-level Communist official named Ji-De (Good Virtue) committed suicide. His nickname was Cocky - short for Cockerel because of a hair tuft that always stood upright from the crown of his head.

Throughout China at that time there were many murders and suicides resulting from political tyranny. Mao's Red Guards were everywhere in China bullying and killing, including our once-peaceful Yellow County. But Cocky was not one of their victims.

We all thought that forty years old Cocky was a happily married man with a carbon copy son. His career within the Communist Party was on the rise making him the last person any of us would have thought likely to kill himself until, quite suddenly, it became common knowledge that he had a fatal flaw. He couldn't resist any offer of easy sex that came his way and it was this weakness that caused his downfall. You see, being the Head of Culture, he had many opportunities to mix with the touring theatrical companies whenever they came to our three villages.

At that time of change, the Beijing Government had been instructed by Chairman Mao to increase the number of travelling theatrical troupes. Their job was not to entertain but to educate. All drama and music was banned except for eight specially written plays promoting the three "C's - Chairman Mao, the Cultural Revolution and the Communist Party. This increase in troupe numbers to twenty-four meant that we had a monthly troupe visit and each troupe came to educate we villagers about twice a year.

Cocky's good looks often attracted the young free-and-easy female members of the different troupes. Eager for thrills they willingly went to the office he used as a place of seduction as well as for work. During his two years doing the job, in addition to new conquests, he had built up quite a collection of previously seduced young women anxious to re-visit his office whenever they performed in our village.

He had a good thing going until his life was ruined when the green-eyed monster called jealousy came to visit.

An older actress expecting to again be pleasured by Cocky entered his office unannounced and found him in the arms of a new, much younger girl. Angry and jealous, the woman immediately reported what she had seen.

In our community news of illicit love could spread faster than a flu epidemic, giving the spiteful and sanctimonious the opportunity to demand severe punishment for the offender. By the time Cocky took his own life he had been suspended from his job, was about to be thrown out of the Party, faced imprisonment for actions unbecoming of a Communist Party Official and his wife was threatening divorce. The humiliation must have been too much to bear. He hung himself.

*

Nobody except Cocky's broken-hearted only child, a teenage son, had any interest in the body. He put it on a handcart and covered it with a sack. On the way home he called on La-la.

"Please La-la, come and sing," pleaded the boy. "Only you can help my dad go down the road."

La-la had always liked Cocky. He had never refused to help whenever La-la needed to fill a form or had a problem. Swearing the boy to secrecy because it would be bad for business if people learned that he could be so soft hearted, La-la agreed to do the job for nothing.

La-la took his friend and workmate, Old Li, with him. Li also had a nickname. Born a hunchback he was known as Cripple Li. He was a bit of a dullard and not at all superstitious. He didn't mind working with the dead and more importantly he had no problems with suicide. To him it was just another body to clean, dress and make up. He and La-la had formed a strong bond of friendship as children. And they worked well together.

Cripple Li was a natural worrier. As he and La-la followed the boy pushing the handcart towards Cocky's home, his slow brain began to form a question.

"La-la, this is not a normal death. Cocky died in disgrace. What words can you sing at his funeral to help him go down the road?"

La-la was busy composing, so didn't answer.

The dead official was carried inside the hut and laid out on what was normally the bedroom door raised off the floor by a chair at each corner. He didn't look as if he'd died by hanging. His mouth, instead of being wide open with tongue protruding, was shut tight. His eyes were half open and his face had a frozen look of deep sorrow and regret.

Cocky's wife hadn't taken the blow of finding out about her husband's infidelities very well. Cocky's shame was her shame too. They had lost much face within the community and she knew that from the moment the story broke, life for the family would be difficult. Then, when news came that Cocky had committed suicide, she had collapsed and was currently in hospital.

La-la ushered the boy from the room saying, "You have done all you can. It is now our job to make him ready for burial."

Cripple Li worked quickly. He undressed and straightened the body, closed the eyes, washed the face and hands, put on clean clothes and made up the face to make it look as near normal as possible. Lastly he combed the hair. The door made a good deathbed so Cripple Li, who was much stronger than he looked, expertly maneuvered the corpse to allow

La-la to spread a large cotton sheet under it and over the door. They then smoothed and adjusted the sheet until the excess hung down equally on all four sides. Lastly Cripple Li wrapped a hessian square around the body, leaving the upper torso showing. Cripple Li, his job done, called to the boy.

Weeping uncontrollably the teenager slowly entered the room and looked at the false face for a long time before kneeling down with his clasped hands resting on his lap. The two adults felt a great sympathy build up inside them as they watched the boy, an exact copy of his father except for a black birthmark under his left eye. This was the source of his nickname of Panda. He had obviously adored his father.

His loud sobbing started off a small group of females gathered outside the house. They joined in with loud wails of anguish whilst their men looked on suspiciously; which was not surprising considering the circumstances. There was no doubting that Cocky had been well liked. Suddenly, from out of the house, hovering above the noise made by the wailing women was the sound they had gathered to hear. La-la had sucked in some air, opened his mouth and with his familiar sweet gentle tone, begun to sing.

Oh on the road, go on the road,
leave this mortal world,
after ending life's gift.
High is the mountain,
low is the valley,
like the uneven life you lived.

Oh, dear friend, on the road you go,
you are now on your road,
your time with us is at an end.
We are here to help you go,
peacefully on your own,
to the Nether World, dear friend.

Though nothing can bring you back,
your weeping son is proof,
in hearts you will abide.
Leave this mortal place,
go well, down your road,
you have paid the price for pride.

We live through the hours you
decided was no longer yours.
Now you must be ready to leave.
Go well…go well, eternity calls.
In your son you will succeed.
La…la…la…la…la…la…

During the song, no one moved, coughed or cried as the exquisitely flowing melodic highs and lows of La-la's voice coupled with the perfectly appropriate lyric soared over, around and into those present. Panda looked at his father once more and stopped crying. Later, he was to tell everyone his father's face looked peaceful and content.

The four men and two lady mourners Panda had hired, placed the body back on the handcart and led by La-la, the procession walked slowly towards the cemetery.

CHAPTER 3

The Militia Commander

Now you are at rest, dear King.
Your face is still serene and rosy,
Just like when you were alive.

Your earthly spirit did sing
The East Is Red.
Following Chairman Mao was your drive.

To do His bidding
To follow where HE led.
Supporting Him you did strive.

Go well, dear King.
Your Spirit is now at home,
La, la, la, la, la ......

The body in the coffin was that of Comrade Wang, Militia
Commander of the three villages. In Chinese, Wang means King. When
he was alive, Wang called himself Big King and demanded that his
subordinates and the villagers called him Big King too.

The procession was taking a circuitous route to the cemetery. Wang
had built this private cemetery exclusively for himself and his own family.

With his burial plot in the centre, the plots allocated to his wife and family circled his so that, even in death, he would be the centre of their existence.

La-la had been instructed by Madam Wang to use make-up to give her husband's face the impression of still being alive. And the first song La-la was singing had already been written by her, to be sung repeatedly as the procession wound it's way along the pre-arranged route to the grave. When there, the family would stand to one side to allow every person in the procession to file past the open casket and wish the dead man a safe journey down the road. During that part of the ceremony, La-la must continuously sing another of Madam Wang's compositions.

All of your living life, dear King
You followed Chairman Mao without fear.
Now you are on your road
Your soul still protects HIS rear.

Go well, go well, down your road,
You are as you always were.
Kind, and generous, honest and true,
Protector of HIM and the people too.

Go well, dear King.
Your Spirit is now at home,
La, la, la, la, la ......

As La-la was singing the second song, each member of the family, the members of the household, the long line of militia men and the villagers passed by the damaged body and made-up face. Most were not there to pay their last respects but to confirm that the tyrant was truly gone. There were sighs aplenty but not of sorrow - they were sighs of relief. Fate and greed had caused the accident that killed Big King. The people at the funeral wanted to be sure that they were truly free of him.

"Good Riddance" muttered many, making a silent mime of spitting at the coffin.

*

When alive, Big King had been a tall, strong, beefy sort of fellow. From about the age of ten years, he liked to knit his brows when out and about so that a deep furrow ran from north to south down his brow. Then he realised that when he also half-closed his eyes, he looked exactly like those tough-looking army types portrayed in war films, so he added eye-squinting to brow-knitting when in public. Then he adopted a swaggering walk, making him appear to be a very formidable fellow indeed. But he wasn't. He was a craven coward, fearful of almost everything, including thunder, lightning, bugs and moths!

Big King kept well away from army service - too dangerous, but the militia looked safe enough. And the militia uniform had power attached to it. *That* was the real attraction. Big King craved power - and the greater the power, the better. So when, in the early 1950's, they set up a militia group in the village, he was the first to volunteer. His size and his aggressive looks sufficiently cowed the other volunteers into making him their leader.

Big King liked to stand out and be noticed. His uniform was as grand as he dare make it considering the hard times of those years. He took over a room in the headquarters of the production team and turned it into his office, nailing a wooden board to the outside of the door saying, "Militia Headquarters. Big King, Commander".

Whilst he himself did very little physical exercise, he promoted the three biggest and strongest volunteers to squad leaders and instructed them to learn army training tactics and pass on what they learned to the rest. The hard, demanding physical exercises and drills turned the inept volunteers into a fighting force that King could truly boast was the toughest in the whole of Yellow County.

He enjoyed drawing attention to himself. Dressed in his best militia uniform, he would march his militiamen back and forth on a village square within his jurisdiction, using his strong gruff voice to shout orders. And at militia meetings he always took the floor, filling the place to the rafters with his voice. But for all of that, he was constantly frustrated at never being invited to join the Communist Party. He always turned up early to Party meetings, only to be left outside like a hungry cat until called to make his report. Then he was escorted out.

Big King's wife was as tall as he was. A powerful woman with arms like tree-trunks. In fact, Big King and Madam Militia Commander were like brother and sister in appearance. She naturally looked as powerful a person as he pretended to be, but it wasn't that which had attracted Big King. Nor had he thought her beautiful. She was a good housekeeper, but even that wasn't the reason. Nor was it her considerable dowry. The only reason Big King had married the lady was that her elder brother was the Deputy Party Secretary of Yellow County.

And at last the newly married Big King was taken seriously. Especially when Madam Militia Commander began "encouraging" her brother to help Big King join the Party. "Look at him, Big Brother," she cajoled. "Big King is the most enthusiastic follower of Chairman Mao, yet lesser men continually block his true path into the Party. Surely you can do something to smooth his way."

And smooth Big King's way, Big Brother did by having the Village Communist Party Leader sent to the far borders of Yellow County. This action so cowed the other Party members that, at their next meeting, Big King was unanimously accepted into the Communist Party.

*

Luck was well and truly on the side of Big King, proving that the Celestial Emperor was smiling down on him when, two meetings later, Big King was promoted to Deputy Chief of the Rice Depot and simultaneously, Chief of the Transport Team. Quite a coup because these two posts offered more opportunities for making money than any other under the control of the local Party. For example, all of the Yellow County grain harvests, including millet, rice, maize and wheat had to be husked in the rice depot. And, as Chief of Transport, Big King also controlled the movement of all the goods coming into, and out of his part of Yellow County. And he continued to command the local militia, making him a very important villager indeed.

Then, from the Central Party Committee in Beijing, came the new economical reforms and the setting up of the Contract System. Big King, by now the unofficial leader of the local Communist Party, and a select few of the other Party members, managed to wangle the grain depot contract.

And while he was doing that, Madam Militia Commander was given full responsibility for the village first aid station and control of all medical supplies to the local hospital, thus raising their status far above every other villager.

That was when they demanded to be called Commander Big King and Madam Commander Big King.

*

From his early days as the Militia Commander, it gave Big King pleasure to order violence against his rivals or those uttering any real or imagined insult against himself. Not only were they beaten up, their money and property was confiscated under the excuse of "the needs of the Party." The "needs" being the pockets of Big King and his gang.

The militia volunteers had a fair share of men and women willing to inflict punishment on victims provided they had the protection of their Commander, making it easy for Big King to gather a nasty bunch of henchmen and women around him. And over time everyone knew they could expect trouble if they crossed the Commander.

Everyone was at risk. Old people, men, women, children and babies. Big King was known to order the beating of every member of a family just for an unguarded slip of an adult tongue, or cheek from a child. And the more powerful he became, the more violent. "It's no point in having power if you don't use it," was his motto.

He checked the Party records to discover the names of the Party members who had voted against his many applications to join the Communist Party. Those still on the Committee were ousted and then every one of them was severely punished. So too was anyone besting Big King in business. Only those in higher political and municipal positions, and those who were useful to Big King, or Madam Commander, were left alone. The rest of the villagers daily went in fear of Big King and his gang.

The Commander was in excellent health, and his greed for money and power drove him on. Those who contracted along with him invariably ended up with a feeling of having been wronged. Whenever a job was offered, Big King was always first to assess the potential profit. If the job was likely to produce a good profit margin it went to him. The less profitable opportunities went to the others, but nobody dared complain.

*

Big King arranged to have some land confiscated from a peasant family "in the name of the Party". That was where he planned to build his large house and cemetery. He then arranged for the land to not be needed by the Party after all, thus freeing up the land to the first bidder. Nobody dared oppose him so he bid a small amount for the land and got it. He then demanded that proper deeds be lodged, making the land his.

Party Leaders use this trick to transfer prime building and agricultural land from State Ownership to their own private portfolios. All legal and above board. The deprived peasants have no rights; therefore they are of no importance. They are forced off the land to fend for themselves as best they can.

In due time the house was built, the cemetery was laid out, and the Wang family moved in.

*

Two years passed. Big King was now fabulously wealthy but his need for more money and power continued unabated. Then fate decided his early death by bringing a strange and unusual set of circumstances together.

Circumstance one. One of King's uncles had spent many solitary years living in the mountains searching for religious guidance. He was not a monk; he was a devout Buddhist in isolation by his own choice, living in his self-built meditation hut. At every sunrise and sunset he sat and meditated, searching for the ultimate enlightenment. On this particular evening he experienced such a strong feeling of impending doom involving his nephew Big King, he immediately set off for the village.

Circumstance two. At the same time, during the evening meal, Big King said to his wife, "I have a great idea that should make me one of the richest men in China. Tomorrow, after I've tied up a few loose ends, I'll tell you about it."

The next dawn, Big King awoke from a deep sleep with the feeling that something was missing, but what? The feeling was so strong that he arose from his bed and began pacing the large bedroom. What was missing? It was important. Whatever was missing was *very* important. Then he had it. The husking machine housed inside the rice depot... It wasn't running. At every dawn, Chen, an illiterate peasant, switched on the noisy machine. So why not this morning?

His wife stirred. "Why so early?" She asked.

"The husking machine isn't working... Costing me money. I need to check on it."

Circumstance three. As Big King, anxious about the money being lost, was hurrying to the rice depot, he met his uncle in the Village Square.

"Ahhh, Big King," hailed Uncle. "I was on my way to see you. I need to talk to you about your health."

Without stopping to exchange the usual polite greetings, Big King growled, "My health? What are you talking about! I'm in very good health

31

and in a hurry to get to the rice depot. The husking machine isn't working. You can walk with me and tell me later."

Circumstance four. Chen was there, scratching his head, his slow brain unable to comprehend exactly why the husking machine wouldn't start. It had always roared into life the moment he threw the switch, but this morning it hadn't. Nor had it moved after the numerous times that he had repeated the process. The long, thick leather drive-belt that powered the machine refused to budge.

"CHEN!" Roared Big King. "What have done to my machine? Why isn't it working?"

"I don't know Your Highness. It won't start."

It was then that Uncle sensed that something awful was about to happen, and it did. Big King quickly strode over to the inert machine and saw a jam of corn stalks left over from the day before. Angry about his money losses, Big King, instead of using the long-handled hook to free the blockage, impatiently stepped over the drive belt. Reaching into the machine, Big King's first tug released some stalks. With a roar, the machine began to move, taking Big King with it. In a few seconds, Big King's life ended; his body caught between the metal and the drive belt. There was a series of snapping sounds as Big King's bones, one by one, were broken and crushed.

Uncle rushed to the switch and stopped the power, but it was too late.

The immediate reaction of almost every person in the village was extreme satisfaction, especially when it was known that Big King had been in such a hurry to chase money that he had inadvertently killed himself.

At first many of the militia volunteers accused Chen, claiming it was deliberate murder but he was cleared of all blame after Uncle had told the true story. Nobody dared challenge the words of a holy man.

Then, after the theorists had discussed all of the "facts', they came to a conclusion that was satisfactory to everyone except Madam Military Commander.

Fact: Uncle had been compelled to leave his mountain retreat merely to witness the death of Big King and be the living proof that Chen had committed no crime.

Fact: Uncle had been overheard saying, "You bad man... So devoid of virtue. You have been called to account."

Everyone agreed with that, but how could his hundreds of victims exact their revenge?

Fact: At about the same time that Big King had been crushed, in a nearby stable a colt was born. It had been a difficult birth that killed the mother. Aaah! A connection. Then it was found that the chestnut colt had defects - squinting eyes, a deformed leg that made him sway from side to side, and a line of black hairs running down from between his ears, over his brow, between his eyes and down his muzzle.

The news spread faster than a bluebottle can fly. "The Militia Commander has been reborn!"

Villagers, dreading the possibility of Big King still being among them, stopped what they were doing and ran to the stable to see if it was true.

Oh yes, they unanimously agreed, Wang had returned as a useless horse, and see, he is kneeling on his front legs, kow-towing to us, begging for forgiveness.

"Never! Never! Never! Kill him! Kill him! Kill him! "

Uncle came to the defence of the baby horse. Being a devout Buddhist he believed in the sanctity of life. All life. From the smallest living cell to a human being.

"It can only be Big King sent back to the villages by the Celestial Emperor," said he. "And the reason for this is obvious. A horse works for man. When this worthless horse dies, the village people can eat it. Thus, all those that eat the flesh will exact their revenge. Only then will

Big King's spirit be given to Yama, the King of Hell. He will banish the spirit of Big King to level eighteen to be boiled in oil for all eternity."

The villagers were content with that.

There was just one more thing to clear up. The local Party Leader made a full report of the death and concluded that, "After a thorough investigation, the investigating police officers and the Party officials agreed that no crime was committed. Comrade Wang died as a result of his loyalty to the Party. His desire to get the machine started had caused him to be careless. Nobody else was involved. His wife and family, in accordance with Party rules, properly buried his remains. "

CHAPTER 4

La-la

Cripple Li was probably La-la's greatest admirer. He never failed to be moved by the clever words and tunes composed especially for the bereaved. After many a funeral he could not help saying, "La-la is a rarity. It must have been the Celestial Emperor who gave him the gift of music and poetry."

Most of the villagers agreed but not everyone, especially not La-la's son.

"A rarity? You a rarity?" Son sneered contemptuously at father. "Nobody wants your job. Only when people need you do they speak to you. At all other times you are ignored like a used rag thrown into a corner. Hah! No one even bothers to give you a glance."

He was not La-la's real son. La-la had never married. Women were not interested in him. Not only did his job working with dead people put them off; it was also his lack of height and his lack of good looks. Although broad and strong, he was no taller than the average twelve years old boy.

One summer evening when La-la was aged about forty - not knowing figures he was never sure of his age, he was walking home from a funeral when he heard the unmistakable cry of a baby. He followed the sound to the foot of the highest of the three mountains and there, lying on hay in a wooden box, was a naked newborn baby boy. He had beautiful eyes, a little straight nose, perfect body and an ugly cleft palate - we call it a rabbit mouth. His superstitious parents must have thought him unlucky and abandoned him.

Luckily for the baby he had been found by one of the kindest men living in the region. La-la took the boy home and not knowing a thing about babies spent a sleepless night wondering why the little mite kept crying and wouldn't eat rice!

The next morning La-la wrapped the baby in a blanket and took him to Cocky, who was, at that time, working in the local People's Commune. Cocky sent for his wife and it was she who taught La-la how to care for a baby.

With Cocky's help the boy was officially adopted and became La-la's son. La-la named him Han Xiao-guang, meaning Little Light but he quickly got the nickname of Threelips.

Threelips was now an adult still living at home spending La-la's money. He had a very big chip on his shoulder, a bad attitude and a vile temper. It was all because of his mouth, he said. It was true that it caused him to have speech difficulties made even worse by never having grown his upper two front teeth. He also claimed that his disfigurement was the reason why he couldn't get employment. "Not even the smallest restaurant will employ me," was his most common complaint.

"Nonsense," said La-la. "You're strong and healthy, why don't you work in the fields?" Threelips stubbornly stayed at home doing very little except take out his frustrations and anger on La-la.

La-la had tried to teach Threelips the basics of funeral singing, failing totally. Or should I say Threelips was the failure. He had no voice, couldn't sing on key and his speech impediment made it impossible for people to understand the words he sang.

La-la was worried. "How are you going to survive when I am gone?" he asked his son.

Threelips seemed not to care. "I don't want to be like you. I want to marry one day but that will never happen if I work with dead bodies."

La-la's heart was saddened. He was now in the autumn of his life and had to face the fact that the skills he had inherited would end with his death. This was his greatest regret.

He racked his brains on how to get Threelips working. Luckily his friend and neighbour, the Widow Yi, was sympathetic and suggested a solution.

"Why don't you help him start a small business? For instance, he could sell pot-stewed chickens in Market Street."

Widow Yi was a street cleaner. At dawn every morning, seven days a week, she swept Market Street and the surrounding areas using a bamboo pole to which she tied young tree shoots. It was not a very efficient brush but it cost nothing to make. She had regularly complained to La-la, "You don't know how many bones people throw away as they walk along eating their cooked chickens. My broom gets greasy and sticky. Every day I have to replace the tree shoots. I burn the old ones. They make good kindling."

La-la thought her idea a good one. Food has always played an important part in Chinese culture and following on from the death of Chairman Mao in 1976 the economic situation in China had improved enormously. And as the people's finances steadily got better so the food industry had grown. In our community many food stalls had started up. They stood side by side down the length of Market Street with a never-ending supply of customers.

You have to remember that I am talking about a time before the American-style fast-food outlets arrived in China.

The market traders had to share the limited number of spaces. The established traders used them during the day and as they packed up and left, others took their places. Many workers and peasants worked on the land until dusk then came to eat and chat under the dim light of oil lamps so, from early morning to late at night, there was plenty of trade.

Widow Yi suggested that Threelips apply for an evening licence when his rabbit mouth would be less noticeable. Even better, because he was selling food, he could cover his lower face with a gauze mask, making the passers-by think he was more hygienic than the competition.

La-la told all this to Threelips, who was most enthusiastic. So, following the advice given to him by the Widow, La-la travelled to the nearest Administration Office situated in the County Town, taking with him a chunk of his savings split into seven red envelopes. One envelope for the clerk to help him fill the forms, one for each of the five section heads and one to pay for the licence. The Widow had stressed that without the bribes his application would be refused.

La-la also paid to get everything needed to start up in business. When all was ready, La-la helped Threelips put everything on a handcart and push it from their home to the allotted space. On the cart there was a stove, a big pot full of cooked chickens, bowls, chopsticks, vacuum flasks filled with boiled water for cleaning and making green tea, some small stools, the food counter, brown paper bags for take-aways, oil lamps and a cardboard carton containing cleaning cloths and spare masks.

Threelips put on a mask and gazed out through his large attractive eyes under thick eyebrows. Any stranger would think him a very handsome young man. La-la was following Threelips as they neared Market Street. A light summer breeze was in their faces bringing the smells off the various stalls. La-la felt so light-hearted at the thought of Threelips at last making an effort to be self-sufficient, he unconsciously began to hum a familiar tune. Unfortunately the song was one of his funeral ballads. Suddenly Threelips stopped pushing the cart, snatched off the mask and turned to La-la, his face red with rage. He was absolutely furious. His eyes spat fire and blue veins stood out on his forehead. "Why are you singing that unlucky song on my opening day?" He barked. "Do you want to bring me bad luck by cursing me to be a dead man?" Leaning over the shafts of the cart he yelled over and over, "Shit! Shit! Shit! Shit! Shit!" Turning the cart, he headed for home.

*

Threelips might have hated La-la's "on the road ballads" but to Cripple Li they were a constant source of delight. Every time he worked with La-la he listened intently. Later at home he secretly practiced what he had heard. He never noticed how out of tune his voice was, he just loved to sing La-la's songs. And he wasn't the only one who loved them.

Not long after the evening Threelips had stormed back home, a ninety-year old woman lay dying. She had been unwell for some time with a severe chest infection, steadily getting worse until she could no longer rise from her bed. Nor did she have the strength to eat or drink.

She had passed out several times, causing her family to think she was dead but each time her eldest son, himself past seventy, reached out and touched her nose to make sure, she opened her eyes and began to suck breath into her ruined lungs.

For three days four generations of her descendants waited for the final moment of her long productive life. Finally, in the early hours of the fourth morning, she was heard to murmur, "I am ready." But still she hung on.

A daughter said, "Her spirit is refusing to go down the road. Is there something missing in her life?"

The answer came from the old lady. "Is La-la going to sing?"

At last the family understood what she was waiting for.

For more than half a century after first hearing La-la's boyish voice, the old lady had been his loyal follower. She had attended as many village funerals as she could simply to hear La-la sing. And like Cripple Li, had experienced the pleasure of singing his songs. In later life she had often said that when her time came to go down the road she wanted La-la by her bedside. "Only when I hear his voice singing my very own ballad will I know it is my turn to go."

The eldest son hurried as fast as his seventy-year old legs would let him but this time La-la hesitated. "The lady is still alive," he said. "I am only supposed to sing for the dead. I don't want to upset Yama, King of the Nether World. He might not let your mother in."

In desperation, because he dearly loved his mother and wanted to satisfy her last wish, the old man dropped to his knees to kowtow. "Please La-la,

for fifty years she has been your loyal follower. She has attended hundreds of your funerals and sung many of your songs. When I was a young man she sang to me, then to my children, and these days to my children's children and their children. How can you refuse?"

La-la quickly raised the old man to his feet. Chinese custom has always demanded that people show respect for their elders, by kowtowing if necessary. The old should not kowtow to the young. La-la had no choice but to agree to help the old lady go happily down her road but first he knelt and asked his ancestors under the ground for their approval. "Papa, you will remember the old lady. She was your friend," he said. "You know I am doing the right thing."

Cripple Li accompanied the two men and knelt with the family. La-la stood behind those gathered around the dying lady and began to sing gently. He had known this woman for all of his life so it was not difficult for him to compose something really special.

On hearing her song, all signs of pain and worry left the face of the old lady to be replaced by a satisfied smile. Without opening her eyes she heaved a huge sigh of relief and peacefully drifted away.

Cripple Li looked at La-la, his eyes full of admiration. "He is a marvel. If only I could make songs and sing them as good as La-la." He immediately began to run the new song through his head, silently committing it to memory. On his way home after the funeral, totally unaware that he was about to be involved in an unpleasant happening, he quietly sang the song as he went down Market Street.

*

Earlier that morning a woman had purchased a live chicken from a Market Street trader and carried it home. "A fine bird," she thought.

"Young and heavy. It will have plenty of tender meat on it." However, after killing it she discovered that she had been cheated. The young cock had a large quantity of sand in its stomach; a practice used by some traders to make the birds heavier and therefore more profitable.

Most people would not normally return and complain; too much loss of face was involved but this particular woman had no such inhibitions. She despised cheaters; especially when she was the victim so she went back to the chicken stall and furiously let loose a torrent of abuse, using the worst possible language to insult the seller. A crowd gathered, which in turn attracted the attentions of the local television presenter. In those days TV was a new phenomenon that was slowly spreading out from the cities and towns into the countryside. As the population of the three villages had increased threefold by 1980, electricity was cabled in and the first television sets had arrived.

With interest in TV very high, the journalist was a recognisable local somebody so when he hurried to the Village Administrative Office, an official was sent immediately to deal with the problem. As a result the stall-holder, a big man with a wrinkled flat face and "fried egg" eyes, was fined one hundred yuan (about £8) payable there and then. The woman was satisfied and returned home.

Unfortunately the stall-holder had heart trouble. When he was forced to back down and pay the money, it was his turn to feel aggrieved because the fine was twenty times higher than the price of the chicken. Long after everybody had dispersed he still seethed with anger until, eyes bulging, he passed out. His thirty-year old son, who was even taller and broader than his dad and nicknamed Da-gezi meaning Big Tall Man, knelt to attend to his father. At the same time Cripple Li was passing the stall singing, "Go on the road, your spirit is skipping lightly...!"

On hearing the song, the normally placid Da-gezi flew into a rage. He rose to his feet, rushed out of the stall and grabbed the hunchback by his collar and lifted him off the ground. Punctuating his words with punches, Da-gezi shouted, "How vicious you are! Why are you cursing

41

my father with your death song?"

Slow-thinking Cripple Li, muddle headed by not knowing why this was happening, hung speechless by his collar whilst being punched by this huge ruffian. And when the ruffian dropped Cripple Li to the ground and gave him a swift kick before rushing back into the stall to pick up an evil looking slaughter-knife, poor Cripple Li thought it was his time to meet Yama.

Luckily Da-gezi was no murderer. He grabbed a live chicken from a cage and rushed back to stand over the hunchback. Slitting the throat of the chicken he painted Cripple Li's fear-washed face with the chicken blood. By the time Cripple Li was allowed to rise to his feet he resembled a hunched up red devil.

The crowd, enjoying the show, fearfully backed away from this Bad Spirit running home as fast as his bent body would let him. Some then shouted to the son, "Don't waste your time on him, see to your father!"

With the help of two friends Da-gezi put his unconscious dad on the cart used to bring everything to market and pushed it to the community health centre. Sadly his sudden burst of fury against Cripple Li had caused him to forget to put one of the rescue pills the old man always carried with him into his father's mouth. By the time he remembered, halfway to the health centre, it was too late. All medical attempts at resuscitation proved ineffectual and the stall-holder was declared dead on arrival.

With a sad heart and full of remorse, Da-gezi, all temper gone, banged his head on the hard earth and called on Yama, "I wasted precious time beating Cripple Li when I should have cared for my father. Therefore it is my fault that his spirit is about to unexpectedly enter the Nether World. Please Yama, don't punish the spirit of my father. When my life ends I will pay for my mistake. Today I will ask La-la to give my father a good funeral so that his spirit is smiling when he goes down the road."

*

Cripple Li refused to go with La-la this one time. He still sported a black eye and other facial bruises. "Big bastard," he muttered to La-la. "This beating was for nothing. I hope he falls headfirst into fresh dog-turd. Bollocks to him and his cheating father!"

La-la turned to his friend and scolded, "How can you behave so badly? Da-gezi has just lost his father. Isn't that punishment enough? Is your hunch so thick that it squeezes your heart? The dead man never harmed you so why do you curse him?"

They argued some more before Cripple Li grudgingly followed La-la to the home of the dead stall-holder.

Da-gezi was back to his normal placid self. Surprised and delighted to see Cripple Li, he welcomed him in like a long-lost friend and apologised for his bad behaviour. He went on to say that by accompanying La-la, Cripple Li had shown him that a kind heart was more important than almost anything else in life. "I promise you Cripple Li, I will never behave in such a bad way again. Thank you for teaching me a good lesson."

After the funeral Da-gezi selected four of his best roosters and gave two to La-la and two to Cripple Li. On the way home La-la said to his little friend, "You are a good man Cripple Li. Not many men would be big enough to offer help and friendship after being beaten like that. Today you earned big face for yourself and for working so hard to send the old man on his road, it is you who should have all four roosters."

La-la added his two birds to the two already being carried by Cripple Li.

*

Of course Threelips was his usual bad-tempered self when he heard. "You are a crazy man," he shouted at La-la. "Do you have the need to be a give-away hero? Why don't you think of me just a little? At least you could have brought home the four rooster-heads. I could have displayed them on my food counter to attract customers."

In our region rooster-heads are thought to be a good omen. People call them Phoenix Heads and believe that they bring wealth and good luck. The stall with the freshest rooster-heads laid out on it usually attracted the most customers. La-la, ever the good man, went to see Cripple Li to get the rooster-heads for his son, but was unlucky. The hunchback had already given them to a trader named Hu.

Hu was another big man; big and hairy. He had a swarthy complexion, a long bushy beard, hairy chest, big strong hands and thick black hair. He looked a sullen brute and that is exactly what he was. He was also the local bully.

Threelips had been allocated a space next to Big Hu. And Hu was well known for stealing space from the adjoining traders and dealing with any complaint with a thump from his huge clenched fist. Cripple Li wanted to help La-la and Threelips. When Cripple Li handed over the rooster-heads to Big Hu, he asked the big man not to bully Threelips in the future.

Regrettably Cripple Li's request fell on deaf ears. Big Hu continued to take more than his fair share of space.

Threelips was disadvantaged in another way. Whilst Big Hu's booming voice could be heard from a distance away, Threelips, with the gauze mask covering his mouth and always remembering his speech impediment, never shouted out to attract business. La-la wanted to help his son defend his territory but Threelips, fearing that La-la would bring bad luck, had forbidden him to go near his stall. La-la wondered why Threelips didn't think that being bullied by Big Hu was bad luck, but thought it best not to ask.

Once again the Widow Yi made one of her sensible suggestions. "The only disadvantage your son has is a deformed mouth. I heard from a big-city student dentist that Threelips's mouth could be operated on to make him look normal."

La-la was interested and asked the widow if she could find out more. She did and told him, "In the medical university hospital in Beijing a clever man is doing things for people like Threelips. Why not give it a go?"

La-la, who would do anything to help his son have a better life, visited a local scribe to have a letter written and posted to Beijing University. This resulted in Threelips travelling the two thousand-plus kilometres to the Chinese capital to spend a big chunk of La-la's savings. Two months later Threelips walked proudly down Market Street with his head high, obviously delighted with the results. His split lip was now skilfully sealed and the roof of his mouth had been altered. Two false front teeth attached to a special plastic palate completed the transformation. With his speech and appearance much improved, many of the continuous flow of passers-by stared, first in amazement and then with admiration. They began to address him as "Comrade Han Xiao-guang" (his proper name) instead of his nickname.

Like the other stall-holders, the now handsome Xiao-guang could shout in front of his stall to attract customers. The first night back selling his chickens, despite not having a single Phoenix Head on display, a big crowd gathered around his stall. Everyone stared at his new face and said how good-looking he was. A few girls even flirted with him - a new experience! He was now thought of as a good spirit worth buying from because his goodness would be passed on to his customers by way of the food. He quickly sold out, tripling his usual takings. Big Hu glowered helplessly as he boomed his voice louder and louder in a vain attempt to keep up.

The following morning quite a number of people called on La-la and Ying-jun, meaning good-looking and the new nickname for Threelips, to offer their heartiest congratulations. The first, on her way to work, was the Widow Yi, closely followed by Cripple Li. Whilst a happy La-la and the widow were chatting, Cripple Li suddenly cried out, "Why don't you two get married and live together?" The two, cheeks red with embarrassment, stopped talking and stared at Cripple Li. When their eyes again met, Widow Yi shyly lowered her head and stared at her feet. The two men noticed that she showed no resistance to the idea.

*

Bathing is almost unheard of in our community. A quick wipe with a cold cloth over face and neck is about all we countrypeople do in the name of cleanliness. Only for special occasions like getting married do we take clothes off to wash our bodies. For La-la, the next morning was one of those days. He rose early, well before the roosters began to crow, boiled some water, stripped to his waist and carefully washed himself. Then, using his trusted cutthroat razor that had been passed down the generations, he shaved and combed his hair. He redressed himself in the everyday clothes he had just taken off.

When Widow Yi came out to sweep the street, La-la came out too, carrying a big bamboo broom. He began sweeping alongside Widow Yi. Without a word being uttered he was confirming his interest in her, and by letting him stay beside her, the widow was saying she had no objections. Then their dreams were shattered.

Widow Yi had a grown-up daughter living at home. She rushed from the house of the widow and stood hands on hips in front of La-la. "Take a good look at yourself," she screeched. "Your dreams are making a fool of you. Stay away from my mother!"

La-la, always timid around women mumbled, "Yes, sorry to have upset you."

That was that. With his romantic notions damaged beyond repair he hurried back to the safety of his own hut.

A saddened La-la had lost the Widow Yi but at least one good thing had come out of their friendship. Ying-jun's business was flourishing and he had quickly linked up with a peasant girl named Lan-hua (orchid). She was willing to be his wife at some future time and her family had agreed to the marriage provided Ying-Jun didn't demand a large dowry.

The newly confident Ying-jun was no longer the bitter and ashamed Threelips. Beneath the anger a sensitive, intelligent and resourceful young man had been hiding, waiting to emerge like a butterfly from the chrysalis. His face glowed with the simple pleasure of being alive and he was always in high spirits whilst doing business. His big smile showing the bright-white false teeth attracted more and more customers to his stall. He stopped insulting La-la and began to appreciate everything his father had done for him. He continued to dislike what La-la did for a living but he openly admitted that the money earned by La-la had been instrumental in giving him his new life and self-respect.

Generally, the people in our region do not suffer from envy. Life is hard enough without adding to their problems. Most enjoy any good fortune that comes the way of another. It offers a hope that one day their own lives could also improve. And the close relationship that had developed between La-la and his son was generally received with good humour too. Except, that is, by Big Hu.

He could not bear to see the once so humble Threelips doing well. With jealousy burning like a fire in his chest, his nasty little brain worked overtime trying to come up with something to bring Ying-jun down, and eventually he did. He commissioned a scribe to write a scroll bearing the words, "Genuine Phoenix Heads Untouched by Bad-Luck Hands," and hung it up in his stall. When people asked what it meant, Big Hu said in his loudest voice, "Clean hands prepare my chickens whereas Threelips (he continued to call his rival by the first nickname) lets his father prepare his chickens. Everyone knows that La-la has a pair of Bad-Luck Hands from handling dead humans."

Upon hearing this, those eating at Ying-jun's stall immediately backed away in horror and some vomited, spreading the contents of their stomachs over the ground around the stall. People soon heard the news, which Big Hu was able to prove was true simply by pointing at the patches of vomit. The result was obvious. Big Hu began to get more customers whilst Ying-jun got none.

Up to that time La-la had often helped get everything ready for trading so Ying-jun couldn't deny the accusation. Of course La-la

47

immediately stopped, so Ying-jun hung a scroll in his stall saying the same as Big Hu's, but nobody believed him. No matter how hard he worked or how good his chickens tasted he failed to cover his costs. He was in danger of being forced out of business.

At home his bad temper returned. He made sure that La-la was suitably chastened by repeatedly shouting that it was all La-la's fault. "Why did you have to be a stinking funeral singer? If you were a field worker none of this would have happened!" Of course, as such people do, he conveniently ignored the fact that funeral singing had provided the money needed to put his face right and start him up in business.

La-la sighed, knowing that this time his son was absolutely right to blame him. To compensate he handed over the last of his savings to Ying-jun and said, "Take this and rent a shop at the other end of the market, well away from Big Hu. And make sure it has a sleeping area at the rear. You can live there and do your business without me giving you any trouble."

It was a good idea. A clean shop was much better for business than a small stall and people would soon stop connecting Ying-jun with La-la.

Ying-jun took the money; over one thousand yuan in small notes saved up over many years. It had always represented security to La-la. Now it was gone. So too were his images of a perfect old age. For more than two decades since finding the infant Threelips, La-la had looked forward to sharing his last years with his son. He had often visualised his happy family group that always included a daughter-in-law and a grandchild. With the departure of Ying-jun, all he could see was a lonely old age, but unknown to him a decision had been made in far-away Beijing that was going to change everything.

Immediately after the Communists defeated the Nationalists and took power in China, Mao Zedong decreed that criticism of any decision made by any level of Government be considered a major criminal offence. That was when we Chinese learned to keep quiet, no matter how much we might disagree with an order.

Not long after Ying-jun said, "Dad, please take care of yourself. I will come and see you during the holidays," rumours began to circulate that the funeral laws were about to be reformed. Cremation was to replace burial with no exceptions allowed. The rumours upset many traditionalists in the three villages - especially the elderly but as nothing changed and burials continued as normal, the rumours faded, but didn't disappear. Our rumours are so often true, most of the people adopted a wait-and-see attitude.

In fact, the change of law had been issued during the great famine of the early sixties but only now had the money arrived in our region to build the necessary crematorium.

At first the rumours didn't worry La-la. He continued to be needed most days. Then came the morning he was summoned to sing at the funeral of a veteran Communist Party member who, until his death, had held an important position in our Provincial Government. His Communist beliefs had not prevented the old man from wanting a proper interment into the tomb he had commissioned for himself.

La-la took Cripple Li with him to prepare the body and was told that the deceased had swallowed a lethal dose of hemlock. Apparently, immediately after his receipt of the funeral reform order, he had decided to beat the deadline by committing suicide. He left instructions with his family to give him a proper burial according to the ancient customs.

The family told all this to La-la, thus proving that the rumours of funeral reforms were true. La-la's heart sank. No burials meant no work for Cripple Li and himself. Oh dear!

The position left vacant by the recently departed government official was given to a young ambitious upstart anxious to make good. He energetically set about enforcing the law and before long the people heard about the construction of a new crematorium near to our villages. This was to be used by everyone in the region instead of burials.

Shortly afterwards a letter was delivered by hand to every dwelling by an official who first read it aloud because most of us couldn't read.

Our community was awash with anger and helpless indignation. To openly complain meant certain punishment so nothing stopped the reforms from going ahead. Work on the new crematorium went on around the clock until it was quickly built and put into service. Demand for Cripple Li and La-la stopped. Completely.

Whenever a death was reported, lowest grade officials known as "Death Inspectors" were quickly ordered to visit the family to make sure the body was cremated without ceremony or ancient rites.

La-la sighed despairingly every time he witnessed families being forced to silently take their departed dear ones to the crematorium. He wasn't sorry for himself or the loss of his livelihood; instead he felt a deep sympathy for the souls now lost because he could no longer show them the road. And he wasn't alone. The Death Inspectors reported that people were totally against the funeral reform laws and discontent was about to bubble to the surface like an erupting volcano.

This resulted in the Widow Yi being arrested and taken to stand before the upstart official. In China the Communist way is to have the police arrest people to frighten them into doing what they are told. Even today officials like the upstart never simply ask for help. They demand it, or else! The conversation would have gone something like this....

Upstart: "I understand that you are friendly with the Funeral Singer known as La-la."

Widow Yi: "Yes, I know him, but we are no longer on speaking terms."

Upstart: "If you want to keep your job you will speak to him again and make the following suggestion..."

Widow Yi, feeling awkward about breaking the ice with La-la following the insulting intervention by her daughter, had no option but to obey. She knew that if she didn't, not only would she lose her job, she would be severely punished. But in truth she didn't mind too much. She had always liked La-la and she loved his singing, so her loss of face was a small price to pay for the renewal of their friendship. The Upstart, after warning the widow to never reveal where the idea had come from, promised that when she had accomplished her task, no reprisals would be carried out against La-la or Cripple Li.

"Such a small local change to the reform laws is worth it to keep the people happy." he had said.

In fact it was an anxious La-la who broke the ice.

As soon as the widow emerged from her hut the next morning, the waiting La-la snatched off his cap, made a little bow and said, "Widow Yi, please forgive me for speaking to you. I was worried. I heard that you were arrested yesterday. Are you all right?"

The widow's eyes filled with a sudden rush of tears. She couldn't speak so she simply nodded. Her feelings about the importance of their long friendship were obviously reciprocated by La-la. She looked at him, her eyes glistening with happy tears. He looked at her. Both smiled. Friendship restored.

That evening the two friends met again and this time the widow told La-la about "her" idea.

"Do you remember the old lady you went to sing for before she had died?"

"Yes."

"Was it acceptable by your ancestors?"

"I think so; yes."

"Well," said Widow Yi. "Why can't you ask them if you can change the rules so that you sing for the souls of the living just before they die? Definitely people will like the idea."

La-la looked at his friend, pleasure and relief showing in his old eyes. "That is a good idea! Thank you for thinking of it. I will go home and kow-tow to my ancestors and see what they say."

It was all right, he told the widow next morning. He was positive that his ancestors had given their support to the idea. When La-la happily told Cripple Li, the hunchback hurried away to spread the news that La-la could sing his ballads for the dying. There was no need to wait until they were dead.

"La-la kow-towed all night long to get his ancestors to approve," he told everybody. "Now our spirits can properly be sent down the road even if our bodies are cremated!"

La-la became busy again and the anger of the people subsided. Only the widow, the Upstart and his deputy knew the truth.

This novel way of dealing with death brought new problems for the living. The time it took for each dying person to expire was different and often drawn out. La-la sometimes waited for days beside a client, singing their personal ballad over and over; leaving him exhausted by the time the body departed for the crematorium. Also, La-la's new routine did not fit in with those who died suddenly such as in an accident, or a heart attack. The corpses were dispatched to the crematorium as soon after the death as possible, giving the families no chance to send for La-la. Also, in winter months, when the death rate almost doubles, poor La-la couldn't possibly attend every bedside.

This caused fierce quarrels between the families, which often also involved the crematorium officials. Sometimes fighting broke out.

After a couple of years of this, Upstart was a worried man. He knew only too well how important it was to the bereaved to know their dear ones had been properly sent down the road but if he couldn't control the people under his command, his chance of promotion would be zero. What to do?

The answer arrived as part of a report sent to him by the Director of the crematorium.

"…May I respectfully suggest that Comrade Han Lao-lao (La-la) be employed by the local authority as the Official Funeral Singer? Before the final act of cremation we can hire out the Memorial Hall to families for fifteen minutes duration to allow a down the road ballad to be sung. At present the cremation fee covers the cost of burning one body. The hall earns nothing. Fifteen minutes per corpse is sufficient to deal with our daily intake and the hire money will cover the cost of employing Comrade Han Lao-lao."

His suggestion approved, the Director went to talk to La-la.

Never did officials visit La-la. When he opened the door of his hut and saw the Director and two deputies, he was not sure how to respond. In a fluster of ancient courtesy he stood to one side to allow his distinguished visitors to enter. The Director sat on the only good chair; the deputies and La-la stood.

Poor La-la was quite bewildered. Here was the Director addressing him as Comrade Master Han! He forced himself to listen.

"Comrade Master Han," repeated the Director. "This is a serious matter. You know that the ancient funeral customs have been outlawed by Beijing and yet we have allowed you to sing your down the road ballads.

"You also know that your involvement in our cremation procedures has caused problems and is a constant disturbance to our routine. Therefore it must be obvious to you that we cannot allow the present situation to continue. However, we know it will take a long time for the people to accept the new reforms so we are prepared to make the following concession."

The Director stopped talking to allow time for La-la to nod his understanding then he continued, "Our great and glorious Communist Party is always mindful of the needs of the people. I have come here today to offer you employment at the crematorium. Your title will be Official Regional Funeral Singer of the Peoples Republic. Actually we are going to give the bereaved the opportunity to employ you to sing your songs in the Memorial Hall immediately before their dead are cremated."

La-la was stunned and confused. When everybody except the highest leadership was pensioned off at the age of sixty to make way for the next generation, he, well past retirement age, was about to be employed. How could that be? The Director laughed at La-la's question. "You are China's last living funeral singer. Who else is there to fill this position?"

La-la was thrilled. He nodded his head many times saying, "Yes, yes. That's fine, that's fine." Then a thought, "Can Cripple Li also be employed?"

"No. Only you."

"In that case, I shall not accept. I cannot leave him alone."

The Director, in danger of not completing his mission and therefore losing much face, said sharply, "You really don't know how to appreciate favours. We can easily outlaw your superstitious activities. Instead we offer you a job with a fixed weekly salary plus anything you get from the families."

He rose and began an agitated to-and-fro walk, speaking as he paced. "We have given this considerable thought. The people need you to sing. Therefore, to keep the people happy during their time at the crematorium, we offer you employment. Otherwise who would bother with an old man like you? Take it or leave it. I expect you to report for work tomorrow morning!" He strode out of the hut.

La-la needed help. This was too big a decision for him to make by himself. Besides, the sudden arrival of the Director and his deputies had to be explained. That evening he went to talk it over with his friends.

Widow Yi said: "You have to go otherwise your ballads will be banned."

Cripple Li (tearfully): "Don't worry about me. I have saved quite a lot of money for my old age. You should go tomorrow morning. I am proud of you La-la. You are now a state employee - a proper civil servant. People will treat you with respect. Your profession has at last been given the status it has always deserved. Please take the job, I will be all right."

La-la took the advice. Early the next morning he reported for work at the crematorium.

CHAPTER 5

Peasant Workers

At about the same time as the Woo family was discussing their own predicament, in another part of the city sadness hit a father and his son. It arrived at the construction site seconds after the lunch-time whistle sounded. On all floors of the half-built tower block workers stopped whatever they were doing and hurried to their lunch boxes or down to ground level. On the tenth storey, bricklayer Guang Da spent a few extra minutes laying the last bricks of a bedroom wall. As he laid down his trowel a loud shout through the funnelled hailer came up from the ground, "Guang Da … a telegram … your wife is dead!"

Guang Da was taken completely by surprise. Never before had he been hailed and to suddenly hear that his wife was dead drove spikes through his heart. He began to tremble so hard he almost fell off the scaffold. Holding tight to the bamboo scaffolding tubes he looked down to see all eyes looking up at him. There was the overseer, hailer in hand, standing in the middle of a small crowd of curious workers. In a daze he heard the overseer again shout through the hailer…

"Guang Guang… a telegram. Your mother is dead!"

A minute later Guang Da was on the ground standing beside his son, Guang Guang. The overseer handed Guang Da a piece of paper, saying,"Here is the telegram. It says that your wife is dead."

Father and son looked at the telegram in puzzlement. Both were illiterate so the written words meant nothing to them. Only the spoken words of the overseer made sense.

"She is dead?" questioned Guang Da. "My wife is dead?"

"That's what is says."

"Does it say how... What happened? She was all right when we left."

"No. Only that she's dead."

"What do we do now?" asked son.

"Don't know," replied father.

*

Like most Chinese construction workers, Guang Da and his son were descended from a long line of countryside peasants. For thousands of years their ancestors had worked the land. Now, because of the ever-increasing land rents and the recently imposed agricultural tax, crop growing was no longer worth the trouble. The result was millions of peasants leaving the land to look for work in the urban areas. Which was exactly what the National Government in Beijing had hoped would happen.

A major economic change was taking place in China. The building of new houses, flats, commercial buildings, hotels and a million kilometres of new roads plus the necessary infrastructure, was under way. The peasants were directed to the construction sites and used as cheap labour.

Before starting work every peasant was forced to put his or her cross on individual contracts that they couldn't read so didn't understand. All they knew was that they would be given three portions of simple food daily and could live on the site. At the next Spring Festival holiday, also known as The Chinese New Year, wages would be paid and they could go home until the next working year started ten days later. They would then be expected to sign new contracts.

The two men had worked on this site for two hundred and two days without a day off. Perfect workers. At the end of the year they would have gone home with sufficient cash to keep the family going for the next year and put aside a little money for themselves. Father and son had artistic talents inherited from their ancestors. All they dreamed of was the chance to carve and sculpture their way to a better life.

Now they had to go home for the funeral and that presented a problem. With not one yuan in their pockets how were they to pay for the train tickets? They decided to ask the Site Director.

By now all the food would be gone. In the huge dining hut every meal was like a war. As soon as the steaming cauldrons appeared, like hungry wolves the men and women grabbed as much food as they could and gobbled it down before it was stolen from them. It was normal to see people fighting over scraps. After every meal many of the workers nursed injuries and sometimes there was a death.

Nobody cared.

And the Site Director didn't care about the two men. His only concern was to get the building up and ready for occupation in the time allowed. He was interested in workers arriving, not leaving. "If you have to leave, you have to leave," he said. "If you're looking for your wages, forget it. According to your contract with us you have no money coming, and there is nothing I can do about it. My hands are tied. My bosses would be very upset if I paid you out before your contractual time. I will loan you sufficient to get home but that is all I can do." He pushed some small denomination notes across his desk and ended the meeting with an indifferent, "Good luck."

He didn't care one way or the other because he couldn't lose. The moment the two men left the site he would get his share of their forfeited earnings and if they did come back he would charge them treble for the loan. He also knew that if they wanted to protect their jobs until the signing of new contracts they would quickly return, prepared to work for food and a place to sleep.

Guang Da and Guang Guang went to the pre-fabricated sleeping hut to collect their belongings. As they entered, the familiar stench of filthy bodies and urine hit their noses, but they took no notice. The men and women peasant-workers slept on bare concrete and did their pissing and shitting in buckets placed in the four corners of the hut. Wrapping the precious work-tools they had brought with them to the site (no tools, no work) in the dirty quilt they shared, they stuffed it into an old rice sack together with their few personal bits and pieces and left.

As usual when leaving the hut, young Guang Guang breathed deeply of the fresh air. He was glad to be going off the site. The work was hard and the nights were horrid. And whether he did or didn't return, he knew he would forever remember that stink.

When he had first accompanied his father to the city, the stench of the sleeping hut had made him want to vomit. He hated having to sleep there. Nobody washed and none had a change of clothes. Just like pigs, the men and women simply settled down in their sty. Guang Guang had wanted to wash but there wasn't any water. Night after night he had forced himself to lie down on the dirty concrete, pull his half of the quilt over himself and join the rest of the pigs. For the first month he had been terribly homesick but didn't dare say anything or shed tears. In this peasant-worker community, to cry meant losing much face for himself and his father.

*

It was another hot day. Bright sun with no breeze. Nothing unusual for the time of year but very uncomfortable for anyone having to walk urban streets at mid-afternoon. The railway station was situated on the other side of town - about three kilometres distant. Afternoon buses were rare, forcing the men to walk. Soon they were sweating profusely inside their filthy clothes.

Guang Da felt bad. After a lifetime of hard work since being put to work in the fields as a toddler, he had nothing. As a new husband, and then a father, he had so wanted his wife and son to have a better life but it had never happened. No schooling for the boy because Guang Da had been unable to pay the tuition fees. Even when it was discovered that Guang Guang had undeniable artistic talents nobody cared. In Communist China, no money equals no education.

For years Guang Da, together with his wonderful wife and growing son had worked the land, struggling to stay alive. Then came the day when the Tax Collector had arrived to demand settlement of the new Agricultural Tax. Unable to pay, Guang Da had left home to find work in the town. A year later his son had joined him.

A bus appeared and they hailed it. Although full to capacity it slowed to a stop and the door opened. They stepped on board. In front of them was a wall of young urbanites in smart clothes. The two men tried to squeeze in. Suddenly a teenage girl screamed, "You dirty pig. You have soiled my dress. How dare you push your filthy body against me!"

Another girl joined in, shrieking, "You are polluting the whole bus with your stink!"

Some boys came to help the girls. They pushed Guang Da and his son to the still-open door shouting, "Get out of here. We don't want dog-turds like you on this bus."

Several hard kicks from the boys forced the two men back onto the roadside. The doors closed and the bus pulled away. The two men stared after the departing bus, unable to understand. Although they had been in the urban environment for a long time they had never mixed with the locals. On the building site it was common knowledge that most urbanites despised peasant-workers. City people thought them the dregs of society, unfit to mix with decent people. Guang Da and Guang Guang had found that the building site gossip was correct but they didn't know why. Were they not as valuable to China as any office worker? Could these puffed-up stiff-necks build the houses they lived in? Or the office blocks they worked in? Not a chance! One day of brick shifting would kill them stone dead. And yet they looked down on those that could and did.

"These people are nothing but parasites," said father to son. "It is better for us to keep ourselves away from them. We will walk."

The two men arrived at the station just after dark. It was too late to catch a train going their way so they settled down to wait until morning. They were hungry and thirsty but dared not purchase even a tiny bowl of rice from the cheapest pavement food-peddler. They would need all their money for the train fare.

"Better to sleep," said Guang Da. "Perhaps something nice will happen tomorrow."

It did.

*

Their change of luck began at the ticket office. Guang Da heard someone say, "Three hard-seat adult and one child tickets to Yellow Station please."

"Ahhh," he thought. "They are going the same way." He needed the guidance. Unable to read he didn't know which one of the many windows he should go to. He quickly stepped behind Woo Song to wait his turn. Woo Song moved to the side then stopped to check the tickets and his change.

"Two hard-seat tickets for Yellow Station please," said Guang Da, pushing all the money he had through the gap under the window. A muffled but clearly irritable voice shouted back, "Not enough."

"What did you say?"

"Not enough. Hard-seat prices have increased. I need five more yuan."

Guang Da's heart dropped. "Not enough? Are you sure? Our boss gave us the money. It must be enough."

"Get away you filth," came a voice from behind. "You are blocking my way."

Guang Da didn't know what to do. He didn't understand why the Site Director had not given him enough money. He was a boss, and bosses knew everything. He stood his ground, waiting for an explanation.

"No money, no tickets." Came the muffled voice.

The same man shouted from behind, "Tell that stinking rubbish to get away from the window!"

It was then that Song noticed what was going on. He turned and looked at the ticket window with the few notes still lying there and into the frantic eyes of the stranger trying to buy tickets.

Guang Da tried again. "Please, I have no more money. My son and I must go to the Yellow Station. My wife has died." It was just too much to bear. They would miss his beloved wife's funeral. Tears came to his eyes as he made to pick up his money.

Song moved forward. "How much are you short?"

Surprised but suddenly hopeful, Guang Da turned his tear-filled eyes towards Song and replied, "Five yuan."

"Here," said Song, slapping down a five yuan note. To the ticket clerk he asked, "Is that enough?"

No answer, just the tickets pushed under the glass. Guang Da grabbed them and looked at his rescuer. Putting his hands together into a praying position he made several small bows whilst saying, "Master, my son and I thank you most humbly."

The men parted. Song to his family, Guang Da to his son.

He checked the precious tickets. They seemed to be in order but he wasn't sure. He shyly approached his saviour and gently tapped him on the arm. "Pardon Master," he said diffidently. "I have no education. Are these the correct tickets for Yellow Station? And where do we go?" He held out the tickets and allowed Song to look at the printed information.

"Ahhh," said Song. "Don't worry. You have seat numbers 54 and 55 near to us. We are in seats 50 to 53. Come, follow me."

The two workers felt warmth flow through their lonely hearts. Never had an urbanite treated them so well, almost as equals. Not only had the stranger helped out with the price of the tickets, he was offering more assistance. They were happy to have such nice people sitting near to them on the train.

Ten minutes into the journey, Song, his wife and her mother knew everything about Guang Da and Guang Guang. They had read the telegram and knew that they were being told the truth. Two uniformed girls pushed trolleys through their car. Song bought five boxes of food and five cups of green tea - one box and one cup for each adult. The child was sleeping peacefully in her carry-crib.

As he ate, Guang Guang stared out of the window without seeing anything. His thoughts were elsewhere. His youthful short-term ambition had been to ensure that the next Spring Festival was a happy event. And long term he wanted his mother to enjoy her old age. Now his earnings for the year had been forfeited and his mother was dead. Only his dream of one-day sharing a creative life with his father was left. He sighed. Hope and ambition were fading away to be replaced by a feeling that his life was never going to change. His father had already suffered years of backbreaking toil without making the slightest progress out of his situation. Guang Guang feared that he was going down the same track. Tears flowed as disappointment and despair mixed with his sadness.

On the facing seat Guang Da's thoughts were of home. "It is going to be hard to enter our little hut and not see her there."

Song too was sad. Those damn discs! When thanking Director Feng for all his help and support, he had promised to do his best in his new position. He didn't much care what it was as long as his little family was out of harm's way. He wondered if he and his real father would get on. It was going to be a big surprise for Woo Bao to have his long-lost wife, son, daughter-in-law and granddaughter suddenly arrive at Yellow Station.

Director Feng had warned Song and the two ladies not to disclose their destination to anyone. Gossip would soon find its way into the ears of those wanting to do them harm. He had said, "It is very important that apart from me, and my mouth is shut tight, nobody in the Bureau or this city knows where you are going. Just take what you can carry and disappear."

The train arrived exactly on time. His mother had warned Song what to expect but the sheer yellowness of the station, made even more luminous by the brightness of the sinking sun, still managed to surprise him. The five adults and one child were the only passengers to alight. There was the Stationmaster, his Deputy and the porters in their usual places for a stopping train. Two of the yellow-uniformed porters ran forward to help these unexpected passengers.

Song asked the first to arrive, "Please can you tell me where I can find Comrade Woo Bao?"

Before the porter could answer Li Lan exclaimed, "Comrade Porter Sun Bing, your hair has turned grey!"

The surprised porter stared at the grinning Li Lan, trying to place her. When only puzzlement showed on his face she continued, "Come Comrade. Have I changed so much in twenty-five years?"

Porter Sun Bing's face changed from puzzlement to surprise then to joy and finally to confusion. He snatched off his yellow cap, turned and pointed. "There Madam, your husband is there. He is now the Stationmaster."

Song had yearned for this moment for as long as he could remember but until the recent crisis his mother had kept the whereabouts of Woo Bao a secret. Now, as he looked at this grandly-yellow-uniformed stranger, he was overcome with awe and shyness. A sharp nudge from his mother propelled him forward until father and son were only a metre apart. Song snatched off his cap, dropped to his knees, opened his arms and said hesitatingly, "Papa? ... My Papa?"

A totally astonished Woo Bao stepped back one pace. For several seconds he simply stood transfixed unable to comprehend. Then he saw a woman standing behind the young man smiling the same smile his wife had given him before boarding the train that took her out of his life. Now she was back bringing with her an exact copy of himself as a young man. And even more surprising, a girl-child was staring at him out of those oh-so-familiar eyes, looking exactly like his always-loved, never-forgotten beautiful wife.

Woo Bao bent and pulled his son onto his feet into a huge hug. Both men were crying tears of joy. The women were smilingly crying, so too were Guang Da, Guang Guang and all the men dressed in yellow. Only the girl-child had no tears. She looked on from the safety of her mother's arms, not understanding the importance of the moment.

"My son... my son... my son," repeated Woo Bao over and over whilst stroking the back of Song's head. Emotion enveloped him. He could say no more.

Yellow Station bore silent witness to the happiest night in its history. The Woo family, the station staff and the two peasant-workers gathered in the Stationmaster's house. All helped to prepare a grand feast that was enjoyed by everyone. All too soon it was midnight and time for Guang Da and Guang Guang to begin the long walk to their home. After many thank-you's and handshakes the two men left, but only after giving a promise to keep in touch. As they began their moonlit walk, everyone waved them away.

Guang Da remarked, "How strange life is. Last night we were in despair when waiting for the train. Now we have new friends - People's Servants whom we can trust. What will tomorrow bring?"

The air had cooled and they felt comfortable as they struck out from the main dirt road onto a path leading into the mountains. The fragrance of growing crops hit their noses, reminding them of the good old days when their complete family could make a living from working the land. Now that life was gone. The Government had seen to that.

In the eyes of the peasants only People's Servants like Woo Song and his father Woo Bao could enjoy life. They had a guaranteed monthly salary, holidays, free education for their children and free medical treatment for themselves and their families. For a low rent every people's servant was given good quality accommodation with a guaranteed lifetime tenancy. The peasants lived in self-built huts that could be taken away from them at any time.

People's Servants are lucky. The spirits of their ancestors were strong enough to make sure that they had a good life. Different people have different fates. Peasants were destined to always be poor. Hadn't it always been so? That is what Guang Da and Guang Guang had been told and, along with almost all of the Chinese peasant population, they believed it to be true. That is why, no matter how bad their lives, they complained to nobody but their ancestors.

Any peasant who managed to escape from the countryside to work in an urban environment was admired. "Peasant-workers make a lot of money" was the common countryside belief. A town or a city was where every peasant wanted to go. They believed that when they became peasant-workers, no matter how hard it was, all they had to do was stick to the job and endure all hardships to get rich pickings at the end of the year. Of course the reality was completely different but the Party was not about to tell them the truth. Peasant-workers were badly needed to ensure the success of the economic and social plans formulated by the Central Party Committee in Beijing.

Father and son climbed up and clumped down the undulating terrain until, in the early dawn light, they saw their tiny commune nestling in a small hollow between high mountains. From a distance they could see their hut and the long white paper strips hanging from the only door - the sign that inside there was a dead body. As they got nearer, above the shrill cries of cockerels greeting the dawn, they could hear much wailing. This was normal after a death. It was a custom that for two days and nights females must gather to cry for the deceased. These women were professional mourners who made a low-level living by moving from one death to another.

When a woman saw that Guang Da and Guang Guang were near she informed the others and from twenty throats the wailing sound doubled in intensity.

Although the two men had expected to see people crying, they didn't know what else to do other than to join the howling chorus. The women constantly changed places. As one entered the hut another exited and went to the end of the line. This was normal too. In winter it gave each woman a bit of warmth inside, and the chance to breathe cooling fresh air outside during hot weather. For thousands of years it had always been so.

Guang Guang desperately wanted to gaze upon the face of his dear mother for one last time. He was secretly hoping that it was not her lying dead. He entered the hut and walked into the bittersweet smell of death. "Mother Guang, your son is here," chanted the women. "Open your eyes and see how he loves you."

When Guang Da followed his son into the hut the chant changed to, "Madam Guang your husband is here and stands beside your son. Open your eyes and see how they love you."

Guang Da didn't know for how long the crying chorus continued. Nor did he care. He did remember being helped by one old woman to a chair where he sat facing the white-dyed hessian sheet supplied by the mourners and used at all funerals. The old woman slowly pulled down one end of the sheet to allow Guang Da to gaze upon his wife's dead face. Guang Guang had moved to stand behind the chair occupied by his father. As the dead face appeared, confirming that under the cloth the body really was that of Da's wife and Guang's mother, the two men opened their throats and blended their genuine howls of sadness with the professional yowls of the mourners. As the dear face disappeared back under the covering, the howling and yowling grew louder.

About an hour after sun-up an old man Guang Da had always known as Third Uncle entered the hut. Removing his cap as a mark of respect for the dead, Third Uncle edged near to whisper, "Guang Da, I have borrowed some money for you to spend on the funeral. How do you wish it to proceed?"

Guang Da lifted his tear-stained face and said with conviction, "I want a decent funeral. She deserves it. It will be the only good thing I will ever be able to give her. Don't worry about the money. After the funeral I will return to the building site and work hard to repay you."

"Me too," interjected Guang Guang. "My father and I will work together as usual."

Third Uncle nodded his agreement and beckoned someone waiting at the door. It was the local tailor carrying a selection of cloths suitable for a shroud. Guang Da chose the best white satin printed with red roses. "In life she always wanted a dress made from white satin with a red rose pattern. Now I will give it to her for her shroud."

As Third Uncle was backing away, Guang Da asked him to take care of the rest of the funeral arrangements, finishing with, "Please make sure La-la sings for her."

*

The hard peasant life made death a frequent visitor, making the village elders well versed in the ancient writings on the correct way to wash, dress and lay out a body and how to organise a funeral. One of the new "musts" was La-la. Before burial was outlawed in favour of cremation, La-la had built up such a high reputation, his participation had become an obligatory part of every funeral. If he was not there singing his songs the family of the deceased lost much face.

For centuries the singer of songs at funerals had been a one-family business, passing from father to son down to La-la. He was the first person to be called out after a death, and as his reputation grew, so did his "territory". He took his work seriously and never let anybody down despite the times when, especially during the winter months, he barely had time for himself. But he didn't mind. From the age of twelve, when his father began teaching him how to sing, he had loved his job.

At cockcrow the next morning an old woman leading several young girls arrived at the hut to make the correct clothes and dress the body. Guang Da sat on the bed, remembering. Twenty years previously, immediately after the harvest, he and his wife had married. He remembered it to be a warm autumn day when he and his beautiful young bride had walked into this hut. On the bed he was sitting on they had made wonderful love many times, but as virgins, their first time had been very special.

He recalled his excitement and his extreme nervousness, and how his new wife had trembled with fear, frightened by the old-women tales that the first time was excruciatingly painful. If her husband was too big and rough she could be split in two. In fact, she said he was a gentle lover and not big at all.

Guang Da smiled at that memory.

On that bed his wife had given birth to their only child, naming him Guang Guang. The first Guang for his family name and the second Guang to mean Bright Light because he was going to be the brightest light in their lives. She had been right. Guang Guang had always been a son to be proud of.

Xiao Ma (Little Horse), Guang Guang's best friend, entered the hut carrying a plate piled high with red plum-like persimmon fruits. This was food for the departing spirit and was to accompany the body. After the cremation they would be left near to her ashes.

Guang Da looked around him. There had been much love in this little hut. He and his wife had been happy for all of their twenty years. They had always been together until the unfair agricultural tax had forced them apart. He to work in the city, she to keep going here as best she could.

Unconsciously Guang Da reached backwards to the secret place where he and his wife had hidden their valuables. Suddenly he was jerked back to the present. He could feel something. What could it be? He pulled out a cloth bag tied with string. Inside was a roll of banknotes totalling 425 yuan. Almost the same amount he had given to his wife during the last Spring Festival. Why was it still here? He stood up, went to the body and pulled back the white hessian sheet. Staring down at his wife he wondered how she had died.

"It was her heart," said an old woman, seemingly reading his mind. "She collapsed outside, holding her chest."

Now he understood. His wonderful wife had saved the money for her two men instead of using it on herself. Her health had suffered, bringing on heart trouble.

For hour after hour he stared out of the open door of the hut whilst the funeral arrangements continued around him. People came and went, perplexed at the sight of the silent husband staring outside whilst tightly gripping a roll of bank notes in his fist.

At last he moved. Standing at the door of his hut he shouted to the heavens, "My wife must not be cremated, no matter what the law says. I want her to have an old-fashioned funeral. La-la must sing as she goes down the road and she should be buried beside this hut in a proper grave. That is what she deserves and that is what she will have!"

Word and rumour quickly spread. Guang Da was about to break the law by not having his wife cremated. She's to be buried according to ancient rites. La-la will be there even though the leaders had restricted his singing to the crematorium. Ay-yaaa! This was too good to miss.

As the sun began to set people arrived by the hundreds. All had finished work early and in many cases had walked as far as fifteen kilometres to once again be part of an ancient ritual and hear old La-la sing at a real funeral for this one last time.

The main attraction, La-la arrived. He had walked more than twenty kilometres to be there. It had been a long time since he had been given the chance to sing for a departed spirit being buried in accordance with the ancient rites. His assistant, an old man called Cripple Li was there too. He had heard the news from a neighbour and, despite the pain of his bent body, had wasted no time in starting out on the long journey. To his neighbour Cripple Li said, "If La-la is going to sing, it is my duty to support him. If he gets into trouble, so must I."

Third Uncle had made all the arrangements. At short notice he had got a special coffin and burial clothes made, sent a message to La-la and had a deep grave dug on the very spot Guang Da had pointed to. He had done an excellent job in getting everything organised.

Guang Da and his son had quickly carved a beautiful headstone that was already in place at the head of the empty grave. Made from local stone it showed a woman on her knees offering her life to her family. It was sufficiently finished for the burial ceremony. Later, more work would perfect it.

Guang Da had sent a messenger to Yellow Station, inviting his new friends, the Woo family, to the funeral as special and honoured guests. Although unaccustomed to walking long distances, guided by the messenger, they arrived in time.

Woo Song and Woo Bao were mightily impressed with the stone carving and said so. "Artistic talents such as yours should be nurtured," they said. "You are wasting your time by working on building sites. You should be carving your masterpieces for present and future Chinese to enjoy."

Guang Da and Guang Guang smiled humbly, pleased to hear genuine praise from these important people's servants.

After a day of hard work by anyone able to give his or her time, everything was prepared. The funeral would take place as the last rays of the sun diminished into dusk. Third Uncle knelt before the coffin and burned specially printed funeral paper money for the departed to use in the next world. Guang Guang placed an offering of food beside the coffin then knelt down beside Third Uncle and burned more funeral money. All around the coffin those attending had placed offerings of food for the long journey into the Nether World. Others had left hand-made wreaths made from local flora to brighten her way. By evening the coffin was almost hidden under many green hues and flowers of every colour. It was going to be a fitting farewell thought Guang Da, proving that his wife had been a much-liked and respected woman of the earth.

Until funerals were banned, this had once been the normal way. And everybody knew that after the interment, in memory of the recently departed, a feast of twelve different dishes for each table would have been prepared. Madam Guang would be suitably honoured whilst the family got big face and those attending ate and drank for free. That is what Guang Da wanted for his beloved wife. She would become a folklore legend, forever remembered.

Third Uncle gave the order to move off on the processional route that he had carefully marked, and La-la opened his mouth to sing.

"STOP!"

A sweating young man, panting from his exertions, raced his old bicycle towards the group shouting, "Stop … stop!" Skidding to a halt he gasped, "The Village Leader has received a telephone call from a County High Official saying that this body must be cremated. It is a firm order and must be obeyed."

Nobody moved. Guang Da stood like a statue, unable to think. Since the Communist takeover in China, not to obey firm orders issued by the Party Leadership invited severe punishment. A woman neighbour, well known for her decency and common sense, moved forward and pulled at Guang Da's sleeve.

"Cremation is all right," she said quietly. "Everyone knows your wife wasn't the faithful woman of your imagination. I saw men visiting your hut during darkness. Others can confirm my words and have stories of their own. Better for you to obey the order."

Her words were like sharp knives cutting deeply into Guang Da's heart. He was shocked to the core of his being, prompting disbelief.

"Why do you say that? It cannot be true… It just cannot."

He moved along the line of mourners asking questions of his neighbours until he was convinced that the woman told the truth. He went to Third Uncle and blurted, "Did you know about this? Was my wife not the woman I thought she was and the money I found was not my earnings? They were hers?"

Third Uncle sadly and ashamedly nodded.

"Then," instructed Guang Da, "we must stop this nonsense right now. Get her away from here… Burn her without ceremony… Send her to Hell!" Heartbroken, he dropped to his knees in humiliation and shame. Guang Guang threw himself down beside his father. His loud agonised cry rang out across the quiet of the evening, touching the hearts of every person present.

"PAPA!"

*

The two men couldn't face the idea of returning to the city, nor did they feel comfortable among their own people. Deep shame and extreme loss of face caused them to feel like outcasts. They retired to their hut and kept themselves to themselves, seeing no one. So it came as a big surprise when a month after the aborted funeral a yellow-uniformed porter called at their hut.

"I bring a message from the Stationmaster," said the porter. "You are invited to dinner tomorrow night at his house. Please look your best. An opportunity has arisen which might interest you."

The dinner was a delicious mixture of twenty finely cooked dishes. Around the table sat Comrade Stationmaster Woo Bao, his wife Li Lan, his son Woo Song and as the honoured guest sat the Yellow County Leader who had banned the burial. He was sandwiched between the County Party Secretary and the Director of Amenities. Others eating included Shu Mei and the freshly washed Guang Da and Guang Guang.

The meal was a huge success. Never before, said the Stationmaster, had such a meal occurred during all of his years at Yellow Station. Nor had Yellow Station been lucky enough to host a dinner for the County's highest official and his companions. However now that everybody had eaten their fill the time had arrived to reveal the reason behind such an illustrious gathering.

"Tonight, it is my great pleasure to introduce two of Yellow County's most accomplished sculptors, Comrade Guang Da and his son Guang Guang."

Father and son, blushing profusely, mutely nodded their heads to show their appreciation for the enthusiastic applause from everyone sitting around the table. Thus far they were at a loss as to the reasons why they had been invited to eat with such important people. They had kept quiet, afraid to open their mouths in case they made fools of themselves or were noticed and thrown out. Now they were to know how the death of Madam Guang was going to change their lives.

The Stationmaster asked the honoured guest to say a few words. The County Leader was a man of medium height with a round tummy, chubby cheeks, thick rubbery lips and sharp intelligent eyes. He was expensively dressed in a black western-cut suit, a white silk shirt, black shoes and socks, silk tie. Normal wear for Chinese officials during cool evenings.

He began by offering his condolences to Guang Da and Guang Guang. Then, as father and son nodded their understanding, he said that he had been obliged to stop the burial.

His next words came as a complete bombshell to the peasant-workers.

"I have checked the records and found that never before has there been a sculptor discovered in Yellow County, and now we have two."

Everyone listened intently as he went on to explain that in these more enlightened times under the courageous stewardship of Comrade Deng Xiao-ping, Chinese art was to be encouraged. Therefore, he was proud to honour two honest peasant workers who will, from that moment on, bear the title of Comrade County Sculptor, with a people's servant pay grade twenty-four."

He looked directly at the two men. "I want you to create works of art to beautify the important government buildings within Yellow County, starting with Yellow Station."

He stopped talking so that he could witness the reaction of his words by the two men. And react they did, from disbelief to surprise to absolute delight. But there was more.

The County Leader continued, "I have given orders for a special compound to be built. Inside a fenced area will be living accommodation, workshops, storage space, a large van and tools. You will have a qualified van driver and two helpers paid for from an allocated annual budget. Out of the budget you may also employ other local artists as and when required."

And he ended with, "The compound will be built near to Yellow Station so that Comrade Woo Bao, the Stationmaster, can keep an eye on your progress. It was his suggestion, backed up by his son, Comrade Woo Song, that caused you to be given this honour. They are your guarantors. Welcome Comrades, you are now People's Servants."

Grinning hugely, Guang Da and Guang Guang stood up and hugged each other before they shook hands with the County Leader and everyone present.

CHAPTER 6

The Crematorium

La-la was very impressed. On arrival at the crematorium, a lady caretaker took him to the accommodation block and into an adequately sized room containing a bed, pillow, blanket and quilt, a bedside locker, wardrobe, a small table and a chair. An open window gave a view of the mountains and allowed a soft pine-perfumed breeze to freshen the air. On the bed lay a white towel, soap and a new black uniform. Black rubber ankle-boots rested on the smooth concrete floor.

His guide pointed out the toilets, washroom and showers and made a big show of demonstrating the wonders of modern life to her wide-eyed audience of one. "This is called a switch," she said. "Press it down and a light comes on." She pressed and pointed to the ceiling where a single bare bulb suddenly lit up. "This is a socket. It supplies power to work electrical things." Down the corridor she demonstrated how the toilets flushed, the showers worked and the taps supplied hot and cold water. Chuckling softly she said, "Don't worry Comrade, you will soon get used to these things. I too had never seen such wonders before coming to work here. Now I take them for granted."

After a visit to the barber and the shower room, a uniformed La-la reported to the leader of his department, another Comrade Han. "I had better introduce you by your nickname," said Leader Han. "It won't do to have two Comrade Hans. Too complicated."

After completion of the paperwork confirming his employment, La-la was taken around the complex. He saw the four incinerators feeding their smoke into a tall chimney. Through an observation window an attendant showed one of the incinerators working whilst explaining that it took about an hour for a body to be rendered down and cooled sufficiently to harvest the ashes into a cheap earthenware pot.

He was shown a large room filled with chairs. "Family waiting room," said Leader Han. "Sometimes it is filled to bursting point and we have to crush them in like pips in a pomegranate." He laughed at his own joke.

In the mortuary, Leader Han explained, "From time to time we are told to deep freeze bodies in here. Usually when there is a question mark over why they died, such as a suspected poisoning or a clever murder."

And finally they entered the huge Memorial Hall. Leader Han's voice echoed around the walls. "This is your place of work. Every morning and afternoon an Order of Burning list will be issued giving you the names of the deceased and any details the families want you to know. Before anyone is allowed to enter the hall, the Mortician will have dressed the body in clothes supplied by the family, or a burial gown purchased from us."

"I can't read."

"What?"

"I can't read. Nor can I write or do figures," said La-la.

"Oh. Nobody thought of that. It's a problem for me to sort out. Leave it to one side for the moment... Attendants will carry the body in and place it in this transparent glass coffin. In comes the family and you get fifteen minutes to sing over the body and allow the family to pay their last respects. Session over, you usher the family into the waiting room before the attendants remove the body and take it to the incinerator. As one body goes out through there," he pointed at a door to the right, "the next is brought in here." He indicated another door on the left. "And the next performance begins." Leader Han chuckled as he said, "You're going to be busy."

And busy he was! He worked hard six days a week. Up at six; breakfast in the staff dining hall, collect the Order of Burning at seven, first funeral at eight. For each body delivered to the Memorial Hall, a worker told La-la what was written on the sheet. 30 minutes lunch at twelve-thirty, finish after the last session at eight in the evening. Two short breaks were allowed for pee and tea - one in the morning and one in the afternoon, but only rarely did La-la take a break. He was too happy singing souls down the road.

Never before had he lived in such a new, clean and shiny setting. The food was first class and plentiful. He just loved showering every morning and switching on the electric light to dispel the dark of night. He often thought, "For the first time in my life I smell like a fragrant flower with a full stomach, singing my ballads to send lost souls safely down the road. If only Cripple Li could be here to share my pleasure."

Apart from doing his own job, on quiet days he helped out his workmates. Whenever Leader Han couldn't find La-la in the Memorial Hall he quickly got to know that he would find him busy sweeping the roads, or gardening, or trimming trees or helping out in the kitchens. The Director was very pleased and often praised La-la to Leader Han in front of the younger members of staff, especially the Mortician. That particular young man was well known for his tardiness. He started late in the mornings and never seemed to catch up, with the result that his work was poor in all manner of ways; faces badly made up, clothes wrinkled and incorrectly buttoned, shoes on the wrong feet.

La-la was definitely not a troublemaker but even he eventually got fed up with having his ears verbally bashed by irate family members. It was almost always the same. Somebody shouting, "We know it isn't your fault Comrade La-la..." Comrade since he became a civil servant, "but it just isn't good enough... Blah. Blah. Blah!" So one lunchtime, after a particularly difficult morning, La-la took the young man to one side.

"You are so careless and getting worse. I'm fed-up with making excuses for your poor work. You shouldn't let people down like this."

The young man turned on La-la, his face red with anger. "What about people letting ME down," he hissed. "I passed the entrance examination to university last year. Do you know what happened? The County Governor ordered my name be crossed off the enrolment list and his stupid daughter's name added. I should be on my way to a degree. Instead, that dullard will definitely graduate without doing any work because her father is a high official."

The poor fellow was awash with indignation as he said, "I was assigned here, out of sight, to work with dead people. Was that fair to me? Why should I worry about letting people down when I am already as good as dead!"

La-la nodded his understanding and secretly agreed that the young man had been badly treated. After much thought he went to talk to the Director, pleading for Cripple Li to be employed to help the Mortician and teach him how the job should be done. He was unpleasantly surprised when the Director growled with irritation, "You people are never satisfied. I give you a metre and you want a kilometre. Have you no sense of shame? No gratitude? If you know what's good for you, you will stop this nonsense. Your age and appearance is already damaging our image and now you want to bring in an ugly old hunchback. Get out!"

La-la was stunned. He stared blankly at the Director for a few moments then turned and left the office. Back in the Memorial Hall doing his job he concluded that the world was too complicated. It would be better to not get involved in matters that didn't concern him or his work. From that time on he kept his own council and his nose out of other people's business. He also stopped helping out around the complex.

*

For La-la, work was always a pleasure. Leisure time wasn't. His advancing years meant that he had nothing in common with the younger employees. He had never learned to play any card games or Mahjong and being illiterate meant he couldn't read the hours away. Life was tedious when he wasn't working. Only cleaning his room, doing his washing, eating and sleeping used up time. The rest of his leisure hours dragged by.

Eventually boredom drove him to a decision. On his next day off he would visit his son and meet with old friends.

Two days later he showered and shaved before donning his black uniform and boots, thinking that looking so smart and different from the old La-la would pleasantly surprise everyone. He walked the distance between the crematorium and his village and first went to see how his son was getting on.

Ying-jun had worked hard to make the shop as attractive as possible. The freshly painted red exterior drew people to look through the crystal-clean windows. Inside, their eyes were first drawn to the spring-like daffodil-yellow walls adorned with prints of ancient paintings. Electricity had been installed in the shop. Neon lights glowed warmly over gleaming glass and chrome showcases. A mouth-watering smell of cooking was wafted into the street by an extractor fan, making the merely peckish passers-by feel extraordinarily hungry. La-la watched for a while, happy to see a steady stream of customers enter and leave.

As the sun moved the shop into shade, through the windows he could see his son, wearing a snow-white coat, busy serving and smiling broadly. He had a waitress hurrying to attend to the needs of the hungry eat-in customers. She was a nice looking girl with a ready smile. La-la could see with his own eyes that his savings had been put to good use. There was no sign of the old insecure Threelips. The new Ying-jun was obviously happy with his appearance and the shop was an outstanding success. La-la, expecting a warm welcome, entered the shop.

Unnoticed he joined a short queue waiting to be served. When he reached the front he waited, smiling broadly, never doubting that his son would be glad to see him. But of course you have guessed the rest....

As soon as Ying-jun realized it was La-la standing before him polluting the air with the stench of death, he rushed around the counter and pushed the old man outside. Sounding like a venomous snake Ying-jun hissed angrily, "Why do you come here wearing black like a death spirit? Nobody wants to be near a man who deals with the dead. You can only disgust my customers. Keep away!"

La-la was wordless. Ying-jun continued his snake-like hiss. "My new girlfriend doesn't know you are working at the crematorium because I dare not tell her. Once she knows who you are and what you do she will leave me. Understand?"

Devastated, La-la blinked his small eyes, trying to control his tears. He hurried to say, "Don't tell her. I'm sorry I bothered you."

He didn't visit the Widow Yi or Cripple Li. With a weeping heart he returned to his lonely life at the crematorium.

That bad experience kept La-la from straying far from the compound. He couldn't understand the complex contradictions surrounding his work. Many people enjoyed his singing, some even spent time in the memorial hall just to listen to his songs, and almost everyone in the region had a spiritual need to know that when their time came they would be properly sent down the road. As the Funeral Singer he was constantly in demand. As a human being he was not wanted or respected. The Director had praised him one day then shouted insults at him the next. His foundling son had always been happy to benefit from the money earned by his father whilst despising what La-la did to earn it.

Sad old La-la. He was an outcast who was constantly in demand!

He became even more withdrawn. He no longer thought himself to be important to the living or the dead. He was employed to keep the people happy so day after day for months, like a clockwork automaton, he did his job. Then, like a message from his ancestors, came illumination.

During a performance one day in May 1985, when the pleasantness of the day made him wish he was outside, La-la noticed that the eyes of the dead man lying in the glass coffin were half-open, looking at him. As their eyes locked La-la was sure that he saw a look of tranquillity slide across the made-up face like bright sunshine follows a cloud-shadow gliding across a hillside. He could only think it was a message from the Nether World when, like a lightning bolt, he realized that only the dead could completely understand how important his work was. The living had no need to know.

In that moment La-la's delighted heart seemed about to burst from his chest. His face broke into a huge smile as he sang an improvisation...

You dear friend are on your way down the road
to meet Yama, King of the Nether World.
We here wish you a good journey and thank you for
everything you have done for us.
Good is rewarded with good, evil with evil.
Your eyes will forever guide we mortals who are left behind."

At the end of the performance several of the relatives, not knowing its significance to La-la, stopped to thank him for doing a good job.

That evening his good mood was destroyed. Not at first, because he was delighted to have a surprise visit from Cripple Li. Unannounced, the little hunchback peered round La-la's door before entering the room. He was panting from his exertions and was obviously in a great hurry.

"La-la," he gasped, refusing to sit down. "Come. Widow Yi is leaving tomorrow and I thought you should see her before she left."

La-la didn't ask any questions. Quickly dressing, he followed his friend out into the dark.

Flashlight in hand, Cripple Li led the way and at the same time shouted over his shoulder that two days previously a stranger had visited Widow Yi. Before telling his story the stranger had explained that he had travelled from her husband's hometown, two thousand kilometres away...

Widow Yi had her own story to tell. After graduation in 1963, her husband, Comrade Yi, had been assigned a job as a primary school teacher in our County Town. The widow, at that time an attractive single young woman from our village, was employed as a cook in the school canteen.

They met, fell in love and married in 1964. Their daughter (the same one who had shouted at La-la) arrived during June 1965.

Comrade Yi was a typical intellectual stereotype. Tall, thin, bespectacled and bookish. He was also a very good teacher with a promising future but all that finished when Chairman Mao launched his Cultural Revolution in May 1966. Intellectuals and teachers were the first groups Mao targeted for political persecution, so, despite coming from a working class background, Comrade Yi was attacked and beaten many times by the Red Guards.

Madam Yi also suffered great hardships because she refused to denounce her husband.

One horrible day a group of Red Guards dragged Comrade Yi away. They said they were from his home town and they were taking him back to his roots to attend a denouncing meeting there. Madam Yi was not only forbidden to accompany him, she was ordered to draw a clear line between herself and her husband. Not to obey meant at the very least severe punishment for herself and possibly the death of her child.

It was a terrible time for China. Millions died, including Comrade Yi. He was stoned to death. Now, twenty-one years later, the spirit of her husband had returned with the visitor. He told Widow Yi that after he had chanced upon the body of Comrade Yi lying in a ditch running alongside a road, he had secretly buried the smashed body beside a recognisable rock, vowing that one day he would find Yi's wife and child. They deserved to know the truth.

Yi and the visitor had been friends from childhood and he too had endured many beatings. Punishment, said the Red Guards, for being able to read and write. Then he was banished to the remote countryside for "re-education" and hard labour. Fortunately he had survived and here he was, fulfilling his promise.

When he had finished telling his story the visitor opened a small bundle he had carried with him. Pulling back the folds he revealed broken spectacles and a pair of well-worn black hand-made cloth shoes stitched with red thread. As soon as the widow saw these things she gave a heartbroken cry and passed out.

As he listened to Cripple Li, La-la's face turned wax-white and shivers ran down his back. A stiff wind was blowing in their faces as though trying to stop their headlong rush to get to their friend. Nevertheless they made good time and it was only about ten in the evening when they knocked at the widow's door.

The widow was not in bed. She had sat motionless at her worktable for hours, reliving the horrors that Mao Zedong had brought down upon their heads in the name of... What? She didn't know. By the feeble light of a single candle, her unmoving eyes had stared at twenty-one pairs of unused black cloth shoes hand-sewn with red thread. Every year since her husband had been dragged away she had made a pair of shoes, waiting for the news brought by the visitor. She had always hated the idea of her darling Yi being barefoot in the Nether World. Now, at last, she was able to visit his last resting-place and lay the shoes on his grave.

At the sound of respectful knocking she slowly rose to answer it. It was La-la. She gave a small sob and fell into his arms - not as a lover, as a trusted friend.

A while later the three friends were discussing events when Cripple Li said, in his slow-thinking way, "At least there is a bright side. You still have his daughter..."

The widow gazed bleakly at the line of shoes. Slowly but clearly she said in a small voice, "She too has gone."

The men were astounded. With one voice they asked, "Pardon?"

"She too has gone."

"Gone? Gone where?" Exclaimed La-la.

"I don't know," answered Widow Yi, shaking her head. "The night before last, when I told her everything about her father, she cried miserably for hours. The next day, after doing my sweeping job, I discovered that she had gone. I rushed everywhere looking for her until someone told me they had seen her, accompanied by a young man, heading for Yellow Station."

"Could it be that young pedlar from the north?" Cripple Li asked. "Rumours say that they were friendly."

"Perhaps. She told me last month that she felt stifled here in this place and wanted a life of her own somewhere else. I too heard the rumours and am not against the idea. The young pedlar seems to be a good businessman and a decent fellow. I wish them well."

The three friends let out long sighs of resignation and fell silent. La-la looked long and lovingly at the widow. She seemed to have aged during his absence. Wrinkles criss-crossed the once-upon-a-time clear and healthy skin of her face and deep lines surrounded her eyes and mouth. Her always-thick luxuriant tresses now hung lifeless, dry and gray-streaked, but to La-la she had merely changed from attractively young to an even more beautiful mature woman and never had he loved her more. Her heartache was his pain too. Seized by a sudden impulse, in part prompted by his own lonely situation, he burst out, "You can come and live with me. I have worked at the crematorium long enough to qualify for married quarters. We don't have to be alone!"

Cripple Li agreed. "Yes, it would be exactly right. Both of you have suffered enough and deserve some happiness."

On hearing this, tears began to flow down the cheeks of the widow. Interrupted by deep sobs, she choked out, "I cannot... I just cannot. I have promised to go with the visitor to live in his town. My husband is there waiting for me. See these shoes? At last I will be able to fulfill my duties as a loyal wife by laying them on his grave. Please La-la, forgive me. It breaks my heart to leave, but I must go." She buried her face in her hands.

La-la understood and despite his own pain he knew that the widow was right. It was exactly what he would have advised her to do. Not sure if he was helping but wanting to calm his friend, he reached out and gently stroked her thick hair. "I agree with your decision. You must go. I want to help but cannot think of a single thing that I can do to make your departure easier."

The widow turned to La-la, her eyes shining, tears forgotten. "What would make me the happiest woman in the world is for me to hear you sing a special down the road ballad for my husband. I will learn it and take it with me to sing over his grave. Then I will know for sure that he is at peace."

La-la nodded then bowed his head in thought. As dawn was breaking he rose from his chair and opened the door to the street. Accompanied by a hundred crowing roosters he gently began to sing...

Your spirit has waited many years
to be shown the right road.
Your tearful darling wife has waited,
anxious to ease your load.
No more will you wander, lost and alone.
See, she is with you at last,
bringing with her your special ballad
to guide you down your road.

The longest river has an end.
The highest hill can't reach the sky.
Your murder cannot be changed,
nor can we know the reasons why.
But some things are everlasting,
Like bonds of love never broken.
The proof is here with these shoes,
true love's everlasting token.

Like snows melting into the river,

your love flows forever and ever.
No need now to wander without shoes,
wear these, with red thread used.
Go well, leave all pain behind,
the road is there for you to find.
La...la...la...la...la...la...la...la...
You once found love, now love finds you.

Later that day La-la and Cripple Li accompanied the visitor and Widow Yi to the train station. She tearfully gave each man a pair of handmade shoes sewn with red thread.

"Remember me," she murmured.

The train gone, Cripple Li and La-la parted. La-la to the crematorium and Cripple Li to Ying-jun's chicken shop. The old hunchback was on a mission and spoiling for an argument. He threw open the street-door to the shop and marched in to stand directly in front of Ying-jun. Wagging his finger he scolded, "Just for once you ungrateful dog's turd, you should stop thinking about yourself and go visit your dad!"

Ying-jun stood still, mouth open, complete astonishment on his face. Cripple Li had always treated him with kindness and had never shouted at him. Then, on the defensive, but not retreating, he retorted, "Why? I have no reason. Besides I don't want to go to that house of death."

"Now listen to me," said Cripple Li. "It was never easy for La-la to raise you. When he picked you up from the roadside nobody wanted you and now you have this..." He waved his arm around the shop. "You must not kick your dad away. Where do you think the money came from to allow you such big importance? Has a wild dog eaten your conscience?"

Ying-jun stared at Cripple Li. He dare not argue, even if he could find the words, because the hunchback was from an older generation. And anyway, he knew that Cripple Li was speaking the truth.

Cripple Li continued, "It took La-la over fifty years to save the money he spent on you. It was security for his old age. Now he has nothing, yet you chose to insult him when he last came to see you. Only an ungrateful shitbag would do that."

Cripple Li's words stung Ying-jun. Never in his life had he been spoken to so sharply. La-la had always treated him with love and respect and so had Cripple Li and the widow. It made him think. Without La-la he would have died as a baby. And if La-la had decided to be selfish and keep his savings, Ying-jun would still be the old Threelips. No confidence, no business, no girlfriend, no life.

Never before had he fully realized how much he owed to the kindly old man he called Dad and he felt shame... deep, deep shame. That evening he had a long talk with his girlfriend before mounting his bicycle and pedalling towards the crematorium.

*

We Chinese show remorse for our shameful wrongdoings by kneeling before the person from whom we beg forgiveness and repeatedly slapping our own faces. Hard. The right hand slaps the right cheek, to be followed by the other hand slapping the left cheek. Then the right followed by the left continuously until we are told to stop. It is our way of admitting our guilt and saying sorry.

In ancient times such self-punishment was often allowed to go on for hours or even days until the culprit could continue no longer. By then the face would be a bloody mess. Mouth, lips and gums would be bruised and bleeding. Nevertheless, if the offended party was not satisfied, the offender could still be punished by imprisonment or death. These days, although we continue to admit our guilt and say sorry in the same way, we expect to be told to stop almost immediately.

La-la awoke from a deep sleep as the door to his room opened to admit Ying-jun. For a few seconds the two men stared silently at each other then Ying-jun dropped to his knees and began to slap himself. La-

la quickly climbed out of his quilt and tried to pull his son off the ground asking, "My dear boy, what has happened?"

Ying-jun refused to stand up and continued to slap himself. Between each slap he blurted out, "Dad, I . hate . myself . for my . bad . behaviour . and not . showing . you the . respect . you . deserve. Please. forgive me." At last La-la managed to hold the flailing arms, stopping Ying-jun from hitting himself. Now very old, La-la was no longer strong enough to pull Ying-jun to his feet, so he sank to the floor and sat beside his son and with their backs resting against the wall, they talked.

Ying-jun poured out his heart. "I know that you have a huge following but there are also some who are prejudiced against the job that you do and despite the thousands who silently respect you, it is the noisy few that intimidate me. I fear them because I am weak. A coward. I have never been able to fight against their prejudices.

"Recently I have realised that my greatest weakness is a fear of disapproval... anyone's disapproval except yours. I have always taken your love for granted."

As he talked, Ying-jun stared at the floor. "As Threelips I covered my fear with anger. Now, as Ying-jun, I still try to avoid trouble. I cannot help it. That is why I treated you so badly. I hate myself for being ashamed of what you do to earn money and yet I was happy to take all your savings to secure my future. I am gutless. A shameful, unmanly dog's turd!"

La-la silently nodded his understanding, pleased to be back on speaking terms with his son. He admitted to knowing nothing of why people do what they do. He only knew his job as a funeral singer. He was happy to have his son back...

Ying-jun interrupted. He had more to say. "Today Cripple Li came to scold me for my behaviour and my girlfriend heard every word. I was forced to tell her everything about you and now she has threatened to break off our relationship unless I draw a clear line between you and me. And as I love her and don't want to live without her I have agreed to sell the business here and open a shop in her village. Dad, I am your cowardly unfilial son. I came here to have you scold me and beat me because I have to go with her."

La-la's hand was gently stroking his son's head. When he realized that Ying-jun was bidding him a final farewell, his breath caught in his chest and his hand stopped moving. As if by its own will, his arm removed itself from around Ying-jun's shoulders. In silence he returned to his bed and sat down, too hurt and upset to say anything. Suddenly his breath was released in a huge sob and tears ran down his cheeks.

La-la's sniffles slowly died away as he regained his composure. Time silently passed. Both men wanting this meeting to be finished and yet dreading its end. At last Ying-jun got to his feet and extracted rolls of banknotes from his pockets and laid them on the table.

"Dad, this money is for your retirement. I will forever be grateful for the life you gave me. I have realised that I never tried to earn your love and respect and ask you to try and forget that you found me. I can never be your filial son. I haven't the courage. I will always feel shame in what you do. It is an invisible demon lurking in my mind."

La-la continued to sit motionless like a stringless puppet, saying nothing. With a muted "Goodbye Dad." Ying-jun left the room, gently closing the door behind him.

The next day La-la went to the local orphanage and donated all of the money left by Ying-Jun.

CHAPTER 7

The Strongest Root

Nobody can tell us exactly what fate is, or who writes it. Some people consider such things to be superstitious rubbish. Others, like the Wang family, have an unswerving belief in the saying, "it is written." They also believe that their individual and unique life-template is laid out for them before the act of copulation, with the writing that settles their fate being written at the moment of conception.

That is why, in 1938, Mama Wang didn't doubt a reading from a fortune-teller who told her that she would give birth to a son after the menopause. At the time of the reading Mama Wang was well past thirty, ten years younger than her husband, and she had already birthed four healthy sons. But that changed nothing. She now knew positively that it was her fate to have a fifth son.

On the same day that Mama Wang had her reading, her husband, Papa Wang, was in the stable tending to the family horse. For absolutely no reason, and completely against his usual hardworking routine, he suddenly felt extremely tired and fell asleep on the hay.

Dreaming was something that he almost never did, but on this day he had a dream. And what's more, when he awoke, he remembered all of it...

From out of a white mist appeared his long-dead father sitting on a white cloud. Papa Wang put out his arms for a hug but was unable to reach. His father, still on the cloud, kept a constant distance between them.

"My dear son," said the old man. "I am here to tell you that my youngest grandson will be born with the strongest root, meaning that he will live longer than any of you. He will be a son to be proud of but for him to age, you and your family must pay a high price. Be careful."

Still dreaming, Papa Wang had no words until the cloud bearing his father began to drift away. He shouted desperately, "Father, please don't go!" and awoke to the sound of his own voice.

*

The fortune-teller was right. Mama Wang had her fifth son at the expected time and named him Changming (Longevity). All four of Longevity's brothers were married with children, which meant that from day one of his expected long life, Longevity was already an Uncle to his older nieces and nephews. And because of the warning given in the dream, the Wang family knew that they must always be on their guard. They knew that Longevity, at certain critical times in his life, would unknowingly and completely innocently draw vitality from those around him to feed his strongest root.

It is how such people manage to live so long. Longevity would first draw vitality from his parents and then from the nearest relative down the line to the youngest. He would then feed off others outside the family. It has always been so with those born with the strongest root, but they must not be murdered. Everybody knew that this would only result in the killer and all of his or her family suffering for a long time before dying. The same fate also awaited any of the murderer's accomplices and their families.

Naturally everyone must keep a respectful distance from people born with the strongest root. And the same happened to Longevity. Apart from his loving parents, he had no close friends. Even his family treated him with cool deference. But at the age of eleven, a friendship sprung up between Longevity and the much younger Guang Guang that was to last for all of their lives.

*

Longevity's parents had joined the Chinese Communist Party as teenagers. After 1949, when the Communists took control in China, his mother had been given the position of Village Post-Mistress and his father was made a District Leader. This meant that in 1957, when Longevity reached school age, they could afford to pay for his education but there was no school in the three villages. Instead they sent him to the nearest private tutor. He lived some three kilometers distant.

Between their home and the tutor there was a heavily wooded area with a path leading through the trees. Mama Wang always accompanied Longevity in the mornings and was there to collect him at night. During deep winter mother and son walked to and from the school in darkness.

There were wolves in the woods. Their terrible howling had always terrified the boy, even when he was safe in his bed. Now he had to walk through wolf territory. It was a place where his imagination could, and did, run wild. Green eyes glistened in the darkness above big slavering howling mouths wanting to gobble him up. It was too much to bear. Hanging on to the hand of his mother, he shrieked, "I hate school. Don't want to go there anymore!"

That night the family gathered to discuss Longevity's future. Their decision was that the boy must continue with his schooling. His strongest root guaranteed him a long life, making him the big hope of the family. Everyone agreed to create a family savings fund to ensure his smooth progress through the educational system.

There was no doubting their belief in his future. It was written that he would bring great honour to the family name, so it was to be education first, then membership of the Communist Party followed by being selected to be a People's Servant. Quick promotions would move him from his village, to county, to city, to Beijing and a place in the National Government - taking his family with him.

Big plans were made for Longevity when he was aged seven.

*

Longevity's fear became common knowledge. An old lady told his Mama, "Wolves are afraid of the colour red. Make a red flag and tie it to a bamboo pole. When you walk with Longevity, wave it." So every morning Mama Wang raised her red banner in one hand and firmly held her son's little hand with the other.

"Come," she always said, marching briskly forward. "We are Chairman Mao's Freedom Fighters fearing neither hardships nor death!" Her resolution left the boy with no choice but to be her brave little soldier.

That first winter of Longevity's school years was extremely cold and snowy. Both mother and son wrapped up in just about every piece of clothing they owned before braving the outside, but they still shivered their way through the woods. The tutor's building was not heated so he and his pupils continued to wear most of their clothes inside the classroom that they wore against the cold outside. Only wet garments were removed.

Sadly, that winter caused Longevity to suffer his first and worst bereavement.

One January day a really nasty blizzard blew up during lessons that showed no signs of easing at going home time. No child who had to walk a distance was allowed to leave without adult protection, and as there was no sign of his mother, Longevity stayed the night with the tutor.

By next morning the blizzard had moved on and everywhere was bright sunshine. After eating a bowl of rice-porridge it was time for snow-clearance. The tutor, armed with a variety of snow-clearing apparatus, began to clear a path. Longevity was given a child-sized wooden spoon-shaped shovel and told to begin clearing the nearest pile of drifted snow. Suddenly, near to the tree line, the tutor found Longevity's mother. It was clear that she had come to take her son home but had not managed to cross the open ground. With the red banner clutched tightly in one hand, she had frozen to death.

*

Longevity became a family responsibility. He lived mostly with his Papa, ate at each brother's hut on rotation, and the wives took turns to accompany him to school. He was given a new red flag. When he asked about the banner his mother had made, he was told that it was unlucky and no longer in use.

In early March, when the beautiful plum blossoms opened to tell the people that warmer weather was on the way, Longevity fell seriously ill. He couldn't pass water and his whole body became painfully swollen. Nobody in Yellow County knew the textbook name of Nephritis, a common illness among the peasants. They called it Piss Poison.

The locals of Yellow County believe that at very particular times throughout life, everyone will encounter dangerous impediments to their life force. Known as Life Ridges, these crisis times are written into every life-template. The dangerous unpredictability of the nine months between conception and birth is one long life ridge. There is another long one during the seventh year. Short Life Ridges occur at ages thirty, sixty and seventy. Then there are random Life Ridges, sometimes short, sometimes long, that wait for people of any age during their time on earth. When a person cannot cross a Life Ridge, he or she must travel down the road to meet Yama, King of the Nether World.

Longevity was seven years old and vulnerable. And because Papa Wang was approaching his sixtieth birthday, he too was at risk. But Papa, still grieving for his wife and worrying about his son, didn't think of himself. His only thought was how to get proper medical treatment for his child. He visited a herbalist who prescribed expensive herbs that didn't work, causing Longevity to continue down the slope to death. Sick with worry, Papa Wang consulted the village ancients.

They said, "Try the skins of toads. It was used in the old days. We remember it to be a good antidote for Piss Poison."

They gave instructions on what toads to catch and how to prepare their skins, then warned, "Be careful. It can kill as well as cure."

At dusk Papa Wang hurried to the rice fields and by dawn had caught six of the big fat ugly grey-skinned toads. He followed exactly the instructions given by the ancients until he had cooked up a disgusting brew of toad-skins and herbs. It looked and smelled horrible, making him hesitate. It felt wrong to introduce the stinking sludge-like liquid into his son's weakened body, so he decided to try it on himself first, and took a swig.

He waited for an hour. Nothing bad happened so he made his son drink the remainder of the obnoxious brew. It tasted so awful, the boy's body heaved with revulsion, but by the following morning Papa Wang could see an improvement in his son. The toad-brew was indeed an antidote for the poison in the sick child's body, but for healthy Papa, with no poison in his system, the toad-brew slowly killed him. Within a week he was dead whilst the child made a full recovery.

Longevity was heartbroken. First his Mama had died and now his first public appearance after his illness was listening to La-la sing his Papa down the road. Neither parent had managed to cross over their own individual Life Ridge - she at age fifty and he at sixty.

Longevity was moved to the home of his eldest brother where he shared a bed with his nephew Ming Gen, the son of his brother. At the age of eleven, Ming Gen was the youngest and only survivor of four children born to Longevity's brother and his wife. The three other children had died at birth or soon afterwards, leaving Ming Gen to be his mother's pampered pet.

Despite being strong-willed, when it came to Ming Gen, nothing was too much trouble for the mother. She deeply resented the intrusion of Longevity into her tight little family. To her, seven years old Longevity was a glutton ever ready to grab food from the mouth of her own precious son. Which was totally irrational. Longevity, four years younger than his nephew, didn't do any such thing and would never have done so, not even if he was starving.

But, fearful of losing much face, she was careful. In front of her husband, family and friends, she treated Longevity well enough but when they were alone she fed the child scraps, made him work like a slave and mercilessly beat him about his body whenever the mood took her.

At learning, being much younger than Ming Gen, Longevity was at level Primary Two whilst his nephew was a grade four student. Ming Gen had a proper school satchel whilst Longevity had to carry his books and paraphernalia in his arms. Ming Gen looked smart in his new togs. Longevity continued to wear his worn out and outgrown clothes mixed with Ming Gen's hand-me-downs. Longevity wore homemade cloth shoes. Ming Gen was given leather boots... And so on. Ming Gen pampered, Longevity deprived, with an eldest brother who seemed not to care.

Longevity worked hard to learn from the tutor - Ming Gen didn't. Longevity passed all his exams with high scores. Ming Gen failed his. Then Ming Gen started playing truant. He went fishing, bird-nesting, mischief-making. One day he sold his satchel to buy a portion of honeycomb. When his father found out, he gave Ming Gen a good beating but it didn't help. Ming Gen's grade-work never improved, resulting in him failing the entrance examination to become a junior middle school live-in pupil. He thought he had been very clever. Now, he boasted, he could play all day.

A few years later when Longevity entered junior middle school, Ming Gen was working in the paddy fields alongside his father. Then, at the age of sixteen, Ming Gen's mother managed to get him into the People's Liberation Army as a young soldier. It was quite a coup. Having a family member accepted into the P.L.A. was a big honour, bringing much face to his parents. If Ming Gen worked hard, he would eventually be accepted into the Communist Party and could even be promoted to an officer. He certainly had sufficient intelligence and was already literate. Most army recruits at that time were illiterate peasants with few brains, so there was no reason why Ming Gen should not make good progress as a soldier.

He never returned home. He couldn't. He shot himself with a loaded rifle when showing off to his army mates. At the subsequent hearing, it was reported that he was not good soldier material and was on the verge of being dishonorably discharged. Everything was reported in the newspapers, making his parents a laughing stock. No longer able to face her neighbors, Ming Gen's mother drank pesticide and died in extreme agony. The gossips remembered how badly she had treated Longevity and sagely nodded their heads, saying that it was no more than she deserved. One must *never* treat a child with the strongest root in such a callous, unfeeling way.

After the initial double blow, Longevity's big brother seemed to grow in stature. Not for him the disgrace of an unfilial and stupid son. Instead he worked hard for his little brother. After all, Longevity was still the hope of the family. Big brother kept his pledge to his parents. He laboured in the fields during the summers and mined coal in the winters, saving every cent to pay for his little brother's education. And in the process, he proved himself to be a wonderful man. Such a pity that his wife and son had not taken the trouble to know him the way that Longevity eventually did.

Longevity did not let his eldest brother down. All through junior and high middle schools he was the top student, to eventually win a scholarship to U.C.L.A. To this day, the people of Yellow County can remember his departure as clearly as if it was yesterday. Surrounded by villagers, Longevity's eldest brother stood on the yellow platform of the railway station, proudly waving his little brother away on the morning train.

Longevity never saw him again. Oldest brother died at the age of forty-nine of nothing except a life of back-breaking hard work. His health would not let him cross over his fifty-year Life Ridge.

*

During the years since then, every member of Longevity's family has gone down the road to the Nether World, leaving Longevity, at the age of fifty-four, the only survivor. He is not yet old but he is lonely. He never married - he couldn't face the probability of his wife and offspring dying so that he could live. What he did do was stay in America and pursue his educational path to its conclusion; a Ph.D. in mathematics followed by a second doctorate in computers. After a period of professorship he was headhunted by IBM and later by NASA.

In the millennium year of 2000, he was invited by none other than the Chinese Premier himself to return to China to join the Communist Party at the highest level and take charge of the Computer Department of the burgeoning Chinese Space Programme. It is a pity that his family did not live to see him fulfill all of their hopes and dreams, and to enjoy the good life that Longevity could have given them. Only his childhood friend Guang Guang bears witness to his success.

Guang Guang has also prospered. His father died a happy man in 1995, known throughout China for his magnificent sculptures. Guang Guang is following in his father's footsteps. His closest friend for many years has been Comrade Woo Song. After his arrival in the area, Woo Song was first given a mundane administration position, then a post in the County Cultural Affairs Bureau. In his spare time he began to teach Guang Guang to read and write. Word spread and it wasn't long before other adults asked if they could join Guang Guang.

In quick time Woo Song had a group of thirty and needed a classroom. He approached the County Education Department and asked permission to use a schoolroom during evenings and Sundays. This was agreed on the condition that Woo Song "volunteered" to take full control of all out-of-hours adult education. He accepted. From then on, in a natural succession of moves and promotions, he was, when Guang Guang introduced him to Longevity, the Yellow County Director of Education.

Comrades Guang Guang and Woo Song were the only people to welcome Longevity off the train - a stranger returning to his home village to pay homage to his parents and family. To his surprise and delight he found a long line of beautifully carved black marble tombstones, each one bearing the name of the person whose ashes were buried in that spot. He walked along the line, reading the names. His whole family was there. Parents, brothers, nephews and nieces, their spouses and their children. Guang Guang told Longevity that one year after being given the post of Comrade County Sculptor, he had carved the stones and put them there out of friendship, adding stones as required. He also assured Longevity that La-la has sung every one of them their own, very special, down the road ballad.

With great solemnity and deference, Guang Guang handed Longevity something wrapped in old brown paper, saying, "I kept this for you."

Longevity carefully removed the fragile outer wrapper to reveal his mother's hand-made red banner. Suddenly, from somewhere deep inside himself, an overwhelming rush of extreme grief took a stranglehold on his heart before flowing through his body. The pain was so severe he dropped to his knees to cry all the tears he had held back since the day his mother had told him to be her brave little soldier - aged seven.

CHAPTER 8

The Crying Souls

Rumours began to spread out across Yellow County that due to the needs of the Party, all privately owned cemeteries were to be destroyed. "Who cares?" Said the people. "The only private cemetery in the three villages is the one built by the despot, Commander King - so good riddance to him."

In fact Upstart was at it again. He knew that a major road-building project was planned. It would take a circuitous route to avoid the high mountains between Beijing to Xian, with spur roads connecting all the towns and many of the villages between the two big cities, including the three villages of Yellow County.

That meant a future profit for anyone having land to sell, so he set out to get some.

Word had come to him that after burials had been banned and the crematoriums built, many city leaders had annexed the now-defunct cemeteries for themselves. Then, after ordering in the bulldozers to destroy the graves, they had made huge personal fortunes by selling the land to private developers.

Upstart wanted to do the same with the cemeteries under his control, starting with the twenty-hectare tract of grave-filled land adjacent to the three villages. His problem was keeping the rebellious people of Yellow County quiet, so, in an attempt to get them used to the idea, he began by first annexing the private cemeteries and bulldozing them flat. And while he was at it, he used the same tactics that Big King had employed and took King's house for himself as a pleasant summer retreat. Madam King, now retired and powerless, was given a lifetime lease on a small new-build flat.

Again the people said, "Who cares? Good riddance to her!"

*

The Yellow County cemetery had a history of some two thousand years. Many of the inhabitants could trace their family trees right back to the first bodies to be buried there. More recently there were tombs where Communist Party members and Red Army soldiers were interred. Most had died during the anti-Japanese war and the civil war.

The Party had always referred to those dead as Immortal Heroes of the State - Revolutionary Martyrs. From 1949 it was ordered that all Chinese children be taught that the Chinese Communist National Flag is dyed red with the blood of the Revolutionary Martyrs. So the children descended from the Martyrs buried in the cemetery have grown up believing that the blood of their parents and grandparents form part of the National Flag - something to be proud of... Big, big face!

Every April, during the centuries old Sweeping Tomb Festival, it had become a tradition for the people all over China to march to their local cemetery and pay their respects to their ancestors and to those who gave their lives for their Motherland and Communism. They spend the whole day making sure that every resting-place is given a spring-clean.

In Yellow County that annual event has created an ultra-strong emotional bond between the graves and the people. It has dripped into their sub-conscious mind to such an extent that the bonding feels as if the dead form part of their living family. Sacred and immortal.

*

Enthusiastic postal-stamp collector, Doctor Tu - a respected traditional medical practitioner living and working in the villages, received a letter from his friend and fellow stamp collector, Doctor Tian, now living in London, that read...

Since coming to London I have always felt that my parents were safe in their Tombs situated in the Nanjing Cemetery. My brother, still living in Nanjing, was there to visit the tombs and since 1949 the People's Government has always said that the resting-places of the Revolutionary Martyrs were inviolate. Chairman Mao himself said, "The graves of the heroes and heroines of our great victories over the Japanese and the Nationalists must always be protected and cared for."

Both my Mother and my Father gave their lives for Communism. The least that Communism could do in return was to protect their last resting-places.

But it wasn't to be.

Doctor Tu gasped in disbelief, unable to comprehend the enormity of the words. The National Communist Government was allowing local Leaders to by-pass Mao's orders!

He continued to read....

My brother wrote saying that the Nanjing City Government, in an attempt to woo foreign visitors to the city, had decided to destroy the ordinary cemetery and the adjacent Revolutionary Cemetery and build a huge tourist attraction. It is for the needs of the party, therefore to protest is both futile and dangerous. Anyone caught showing dissent or speaking out against the decision will be arrested and severely punished.

Doctor Tu was appalled. If the cemeteries were being destroyed in the cities, it was only a matter of time before the same thing happened in Yellow County.

He was right. The Upstart issued the official order in March; three weeks before the Sweeping Tomb Festival was due to begin. It said that the expenses involved in the necessary opening of the graves, the removal of the human remains and all cremations must be paid for by the relatives of the dead. And the work must be completed within one month. The bulldozers would destroy all graves and remains not moved by the deadline of April the 15th!

The people rose up as one to protest. A march around the three villages was quickly organised but someone reported it to the authorities. A company of Red Army Soldiers brought in to quell any civil disobedience ruthlessly broke up the march. The result was five of the marchers killed, many others wounded and lots of arrests.

The villagers decided to occupy the cemetery. That too resulted in more deaths, more wounded and lots more arrests.

Most of the arrested "criminals" were given long prison sentences with hard labour. The rest were shot. That is the way dissent is dealt with in Communist China. The Leaders are always right and the protesters are always wrong.

There were no more mass protests.

*

Four bulldozers, four mechanical diggers, four cranes, four huge trucks, four fuel tankers and another company of soldiers arrived by special night-train. By dawn the next day the machinery was in place, waiting to be used. At each corner of the cemetery a squad of soldiers guarded one bulldozer, one digger, one crane, one truck and one fuel tanker.

Each quarter of the cemetery had a name. The northwest quarter was known as Plum Blossom Hill. The northeast quarter contained the Revolutionary Tombs so it was simply named Immortal. The southwest quarter was called Wild Flower Terrace and the southeast section was known as Respect.

But there was no respect for the dead. Not even for the heroes. A few prominent non-party citizens wrote to Beijing asking for help. The reply they received was that the National Government would not interfere in local cemetery affairs; contact your local Governing Body.

A week later those citizens who had put their names to the letter, including Doctor Tu, were arrested, tried and jailed.

Clearly all levels of the Communist Leadership no longer had any interest in the dead. "Make Money" was the new mantra.

*

The people were allowed to begin grave-digging on the day of the Sweeping Tomb Festival. From the outset it rained continuously, filling the holes with water. Digging by people armed only with hand-tools was near impossible but it had to be done. Every request to the military for help by using the diggers was rudely refused. The big machines remained idle throughout the whole month.

Some families had several hundred ancestors buried there, and despite every available family member coming in by train from all corners of China, progress was slow. Some cursed the rain. Others kow-towed beside the graves, pleading for help from their ancestors. "Please, it is not us. It is the Party. We are under orders to disturb your sleep. Why can't you help us?"

The digging continued by day and by night but progress was slow. A rumour began to circulate that the dead did not agree with being moved out of their graves and in a bid to stop the work, the crying souls turned their tears to heavy rain.

Many people believed this and collected the rainwater. Some simply drank it. Many people took home fragments of clothing, bone, hair, teeth and the water to create a private family shrine.

It continued to rain.

Despite the difficulties, a steady stream of cardboard coffins (sold at a good profit by the Upstart organisation) were filled at the cemetery, delivered to the crematorium and stacked up in twenties in the open air to await the ovens. Everywhere there was the stink of rotting flesh.

*

La-la was at his wits end. He too believed that the souls were crying but he was powerless to help. Despite him having a thousand years of past Funeral Singers buried in the cemetery, he had been specifically ordered by the Director not to go there or interfere with what was going on. The best he could do was sing to the stacks of stinking coffins. At every available moment he walked up and down in the pouring rain singing his made-up songs.

This was a new thing for him. He had always sung for the dying and recently dead, guiding their spirits happily down the road. Now he was helping bring peace to those poor souls that had been dragged back from under the ground. He didn't know if he was doing right or wrong. He simply felt that he should do whatever he could to help them find their way back to their proper place.

*

In the crematorium the contents of the coffins attracted a motley collection of carrion-eating birds. They easily ripped open the thin, damp cardboard to get at what was inside. The greedy squabbling birds soon created a mess, with thousands of bits of dead people spread out in all directions on the ground, with more bits left on every stack of coffins.

Rats swarmed all over the coffins, eating the contents and dragging other bits away to their nests. It was horrendous.

In the cemetery it was much worse. In addition to the birds and rats, thousands of four legged animals foraged among the graves and fought over whatever was there. It was really too dangerous for people to continue digging, but they did. As they dug, wild dogs and wolves waited to snatch whatever was unearthed, and attacked the diggers trying to stop them.

At last it was April 16th. With almost every inhabitant of the three villages watching, the four bulldozers fired up and moved into the cemetery and began to smash everything to bits. There was still a large number of untouched graves together with all of the paraphernalia that the living use to prove their love, loyalty and respect for their dead.

Steadily and methodically the bulldozers smashed down the memorial stones, statues, small pagodas, tombs and everything else that stood in their way. For the watchers, it was really the first proper realization of what was happening. Up to that point they had been too busy to take in the loss of their culture. Now, before their eyes, everything to do with their ancestors, and therefore the roots of their very existence on earth, was being obliterated.

As one, the people dropped onto their knees and from out of their mouths erupted sounds that are most commonly associated with torture victims. Of bodies being ripped apart. But it wasn't their bodies. It was the sound of their inner selves being destroyed. It was then that the inhabitants of the villages entered into a period of deep mourning.

And the rain continued to fall.

*

After the bulldozers had finished their work, along came the soldiers. With canisters strapped to their backs they walked forward and sprayed the whole area with diesel fuel. Then they lit fires to burn across the whole of the cemetery.

After the fires, the stink disappeared along with the smoke. Then the diggers used their huge shovels to lift off the topsoil together with all of the grave-debris and load it onto the trucks. The cranes were used to lift any heavy item and put it on a truck.

When loaded, the trucks drove off to Yellow Station and tipped their loads into railway wagons. They, in turn, were hooked up to the local trains and taken away.

For the return journey to the cemetery, the trucks were loaded with topsoil to be spread out over the cemetery area.

A week after the fires, all traces of the cemetery had disappeared, leaving a vast tract of usable, very valuable land.

That was what Upstart had annexed for himself.

CHAPTER 9

Murder

Away from the cemetery, life continued much as normal. Shops opened, shoppers shopped, traders traded, babies were born and other people died - with one of the deaths proving to be a murder.

It was a mundane sort of murder. Young wife desiring more from life finds a strapping young lover and the two of them dispose of the older husband.

The murdered husband, Comrade Ling Wang, was a forty-six years old dentist. His wife, twenty-seven years old Lixia and her twenty-one years old lover Yang, committed the crime.

The lovers, both illiterate and not too bright, decided that it would be an easy kill. Bash husband over the head with a heavy iron skillet, place the body in a closet but leave the door open, then set fire to the small jerry-built semi-detached bungalow. Yang would leave Lixia to start the fire. She would get the fire going before running from the house screaming for help. The fire would burn the body, but even if it didn't, it would appear to be an unfortunate accident, with hubby hiding in the closet to escape the flames but dying anyway.

Simple!

And before the police detective arrived, the local police, already preoccupied with what was happening in the cemetery, did come to this easy conclusion. What ruined the plan was that the fire also consumed the bungalow next door, killing two people. The death toll might have been higher if the rain hadn't kept the fire from spreading.

This took the interest of the top Yellow County homicide detective and it was he who had come in by train to nose around for a few days before stating, quite categorically, that it was murder.

That was sufficient for the local police. If the top detective said it was murder, then it was murder, so, without really knowing why, they arrested the lovers and had them up before the three judges the very next morning.

The prosecution case hinged upon the evidence presented by the detective...

The lovers were known to the gossips. And the gossips were only too pleased to be involved in a death, so every tasty gossipy titbit was revealed.

Lixia claimed that she was in bed when she smelled smoke and ran from the bungalow in her nightclothes.

There was only one bed in the home and it hadn't been slept in.

The fire had been started in the centre of the living area. In the corner of the room was a screw-top jar containing a small amount of petrol.

The autopsy, simple as it was, had reported that the fire or falling debris did not cause the blow to the rear of the deceased head. Indeed, the body tucked away in the closet was well protected from the worst of the fire.

There was very little debris near to the body.

The lungs were clear of smoke.

The conclusion could only be that the husband was dead before being placed in the closet.

A search of Yang's hut revealed a packed bag containing Lixia's best clothes, underwear, make up and jewellery.

Yang had on his person a wad of money. When asked, he could not adequately explain where it had come from.

The gossips knew that the dentist kept money in the bungalow.

No money was found in the bungalow.

After strong questioning and more than a little physical pain, Yang broke. Hoping for a lenient punishment he said that it was all Lixia's idea and she had started the fire.

Lixia admitted starting the fire but said Yang had killed her husband and placed him in the closet.

Yang said that both of them had put the body in the closet.

*

The court provided a defence lawyer from a list of lawyers retained for this purpose. They never win a case because the Party is always right. Even without the overwhelming evidence, the pair would have been found guilty because The State was also the accuser - and in China, The State is never, ever wrong.

No defence was presented.

*

The court proceedings took less than an hour to arrive at a guilty verdict for one count of murder and two counts of manslaughter and the pair were sentenced to death.

It was now mid-morning.

To allow for any last-minute defence evidence to be discovered and presented, the pair would die at three that same afternoon.

In attendance at the execution was a flatbed truck, an ambulance, two nurses, a doctor, the mortician based at the Crematorium and the Crematorium Director. Also there was the executioner armed with two high-calibre revolvers, a judge to read out the guilty verdict and several men detailed to move the bodies and clean up afterwards.

One prisoner is shot in the back of the head and the body carried into the ambulance to have every useful organ removed before being placed into a cardboard coffin. The coffin is then put onto the flatbed truck.

Prisoners have no rights. The leaders decide what happens to the body.

The second prisoner is shot and the organs harvested.

The ambulance, carrying the doctor, the nurses and the organs is the first vehicle to leave the area, siren blaring. The organs will be sold to the highest bidders needing a transplant. The coffins are taken to the crematorium ovens and everyone else leaves the area.

Execution, Chinese style.

CHAPTER 10

Panda

Flanked by his bodyguards the Town Mayor moved forward to address the people crowded into the Memorial Hall. So many had turned up, those unable to get into the hall waited outside to listen to the loudspeakers. Mingling with the people both inside and out were television and newspaper reporters out to get a different slant on this story.

The Mayor didn't mind the lenses focused on him. He hoped to see himself on the television news that evening, but goodness, he was nervous! He had never before had to officiate at such a high profile funeral as this.

Up to yesterday, the hated Upstart had intended to be where the Mayor was now.

"Too bold," said the people. "He had better not show his face around here!"

Fearful of a riot and personal injury, Upstart ordered the local Mayor to do the job.

Conscious of the lenses and fearful of making a fool of himself, the Mayor stepped forward and stood in front of the coffin. It was now time for La-la to sing his ballad. Everyone listened, marvelling at the voice gloriously sending this special man down his road.

Ballad ended, the Mayor read his prepared speech.

Comrades, we are here today to bid farewell to a brave man, but sadly I cannot tell you his name, nor can I tell you in what part of our glorious motherland he was born. In fact, I know nothing about him. He is a mystery... An enigma... An unknown hero.

The Mayor stopped talking to clear his throat before continuing.

So what do we call him? Surely not Comrade X. He deserves better than that. Should it be Comrade No Name? No, that is not good enough either. This man deserves our respect, so I propose to give him the name of a famous Chinese warrior king. Therefore comrades, in this glass coffin lies the body of our very own Comrade Jin-gang. And as we all know, Jin-gang is the chosen Guardian of the Gates to the Nether World. In Chinese mythology, no other warrior is more important. It is a fitting name for our unknown hero.

He paused, waiting for someone to disagree. When nobody did, he continued,

As we all know, at just after dusk on the 1ˢᵗ of April, Comrade Jin-gang, a complete stranger to our three villages, with no thought for his own safety, three times rushed into the well-alight Pu home to save lives.

He didn't know that in the adjoining property a murdering wife had deliberately started the fire. All Jin-gang knew was that people needed help and it is entirely due to him that seven years old Pu Lin, her twin sister Pu Ling, and Mother Pu, are still alive. Sadly, whilst trying to save the life of Father Pu - an invalid, Comrade Jin-gang sacrificed his own life. When the bodies were found just a short distance from safety, Father Pu was still clinging to Comrade Jin-gang. The fire had touched neither body. Death was by smoke inhalation.

As you know, Father Pu's funeral took place last month. We had hoped to do a joint funeral but couldn't because the man who had saved three lives was not known... And he still isn't, despite repeated radio, press and television appeals for information. So here we are, gathered to say our goodbyes to a heroic stranger.

The Mayor picked up a short pointer before continuing.

I have had a chance to look carefully at this man whom we now call Comrade Jin-gang. Aged in his late thirties, he was a clean and neat man. Using the pointer the Mayor continued, His hair was neatly cut, his fingernails were trimmed, he was clean-shaven, his good-quality shoes were polished to a bright shine and his suit was cut from good cloth. And see, there are the four corners of a handkerchief peeping out from the top pocket of his jacket.

The Mayor put aside the pointer before continuing...

Without doubt he was a Loyal Communist Party member but strangely he had not a shred of identification on him, nor any keys or money. The fine clothes he was wearing helped not a jot. There is no maker's name or labels. That is why we have no idea who Jin-gang is or what he did to earn his money. All we know is that he was a good man... A loyal and brave Communist. So, Comrade Jin-gang, I bid you a respectful goodbye from all of us who live in the three villages. You are a true Communist hero.

*

There is more to this story...

The day before the "Jin-gang" memorial farewell, the Crematorium Director sought out La-la saying, "Comrade La-la, I have an urgent job for you. I want you to assist the Mortician with a very important body. It must be prepared and dressed as impeccably as possible, ready for a memorial meeting tomorrow morning. And I want you to sing one of your very best down the road ballads too."

La-la was puzzled. Why had the Director ordered him to assist the Mortician after banning him from going near the Mortuary? And why must he sing a best quality ballad?

The Mortician had the answers. "This body really is unique. He's the unknown man who ran into the burning building and died trying to save the invalid. Remember him?"

"Ah, yes!" Exclaimed La-la. "Didn't they try everything to discover his name but couldn't?"

"Correct. And now they want to turn him into a Communist Party Hero... A true example of bravery for the people to follow. Actually, it's to take the people's thoughts away from the cemetery by saying, "look how wonderful we Communists really are."

"So where is the body?"

"On it's way."

*

Accompanied by the Director, the body arrived. La-la took one look and exclaimed, "I know who this is... It's Panda!"

The Director shouted, *"WHAT!"*

"See the birthmark on his face? It's Panda, son of Cocky."

The Director looked very uncomfortable. "La-la, are you sure?"

"Positive," asserted La-la. "Cocky was before your time. He hanged himself, leaving a wife and Panda, his teenage son. They left the area soon after the funeral. Cocky was a medium grade Party cadre but I heard that Panda never tried to join the Communist Party."

"Who told you that!" Sneered the Director.

"Cripple Li... Two days ago."

Moving out of earshot of the Mortician, the Director sat on a chair and with a deep sigh, said, "You'd better tell me about it."

"Well," said La-la. "I visited Cripple Li and he told me that Panda paid him a visit. It seems that news of the destruction of our cemetery has spread far and wide. Panda heard about it and came back by train to check on the graves of his dad and his ancestors."

"And...?" said the Director.

"The graves were still untouched so Panda kow-towed to his ancestors, asking them to forgive him for not being able to spend more time with them. He was soon to leave China for France. A snakehead had made all the arrangements. He could carry his money but he mustn't have any identifying papers on him. The snakehead would give him false papers at Beijing airport."

"And...?" repeated the Director, becoming impatient.

"After leaving the cemetery, Panda came looking for me but, of course, I wasn't there, so he sought out Cripple Li. He wanted to pay Cripple Li and me for our services all those years ago when we helped send his dad safely down the road.

"Cripple Li told me that Panda was dressed in shabby clothes, so he was surprised when Panda produced a big roll of banknotes from a money-belt and peeled off a 100-yuan note for each of us. I've still got mine in my pocket... Look."

La-la stopped talking to reach into his pocket and pull out a 100-yuan banknote. Replacing it, he continued...

"Cripple Li said that Panda noticed Cripple Li's funny looks and explained that after his mother died, he travelled south to the city of Shenzhen. He had no money and with Shenzhen being much warmer in winter, he thought he could survive better there. But he had no registration for Shenzhen so he had to live hand to mouth as best he could.

"Then he joined a criminal gang that stole anything they could get their hands on, and in due course he became their leader. He made loads of money, which he saved until he had enough to buy his way out of China with plenty left over for a new start in Europe."

"Hmmm." Murmured the Director. "The Leaders have made big plans for this body. The clothes he'll be wearing will be of good quality, so you do the best you can for your friend Panda - make him look good. But I warn you. Don't you ever dare say anything to anybody about what you know. You'll probably be shot. The names of Cocky and Panda must remain in the past. Understand?"

Not understanding but cowed by the thought of being shot, La-la nodded his head, saying, "Yes. I understand."

The Director stood up. "Good. And you tell Cripple Li to keep his mouth shut too."

"I wonder what happened to his money." Queried La-la.

"Who knows?" replied the Director. "It's none of our business so you'd better forget about that too."

CHAPTER 11

La-la.

Empty unhappy weeks and months went by. La-la continued to endure his isolated island-like existence within the busy compound, prompting him to take long walks in the mountains when off duty. During a particularly strong bout of loneliness he made an unplanned journey back to his village. It was now 1991 and the community he had known for all of his life had all but disappeared to be replaced by a small town. At last there was a school, albeit exclusively for the children of Communist Party members, and a decent medical centre with a hospital. Next to the medical centre was an army barracks.

The changes were a big surprise but what brought big lonely tears was the sight of grey concrete blocks of flats standing where his, the widow's and Cripple Li's huts had been. His old life had completely disappeared, adding to his sense of being cut off from humankind. He stood for a long time staring at everything, understanding nothing, feeling like an outsider, an intruder.

Suddenly a familiar voice. "La-la, how good it is to see you!" From the flats a smiling Cripple Li looked down from a second floor window. "Come up."

Cripple Li proudly ushered La-la into the little flat. They entered directly into a small kitchen complete with running cold water from a tap and a small two-ring electric stove. A large aluminium kettle sat on top of the stove and to the side was the always-essential double-sized vacuum flask. We Chinese have always had to boil our drinking water and we still do. On wooden shelves, pots, pans, crockery, utensils and chopsticks were neatly laid out.

Off the kitchen was a small toilet, empty except for some newspaper squares and a bucket filled with water standing beside a hole let into the concrete. Users had to squat over the hole to do what they had to do. When finished they used water from the bucket to flush.

Cripple Li led the way from the kitchen into a good-size room used for living and sleeping. A small bed in the corner, an old armchair, a table with two chairs beside the window, an old wooden chest of drawers in one corner and hooks to hang clothes in another. A new white plastic radio sat on a wooden packing case and an electric heater warmed the room. Everything was spotlessly clean.

"I was given this place when they took away my old home," Cripple Li was saying. "It is much better here but not so friendly. I miss the old life."

"Me too," replied La-la. "I feel like a fish out of water these days. I don't belong in the crematorium and today I find that I no longer have a home here."

Cripple Li made cups of green tea and the two pals settled down for a "remember when" chat. After that meeting La-la frequently visited Cripple Li. It helped dispel his constant loneliness.

*

Chairman Mao had died in 1976, to be briefly followed by the useless Hua Guo-feng. Then dynamic Deng Xiao-Ping took over as leader. He introduced a completely new range of political and financial reforms that resulted in a steadily improving economic situation. The Deng reforms were carried forward by his successor, Jiang Ze-min. By the early nineties China had entered into a period of economic prosperity.

In the town, roads were laid and lined with shops and stores. Parks and recreational areas had been created and the street market had doubled in size. The traders had done very well. Most no longer used handcarts;

they had vans and small pick-up trucks. The market area had been levelled and electric lights had replaced oil lamps. Big Hu now had a half interest in several stalls run by members of his family and he ran his various business interests from the shop once occupied by Ying-jun.

He was still the king of the market but age had steadily crept up, making him the target for younger rivals. Although Big Hu was a bully, he was no coward. He had never backed away from a good scrap and so far was unbeaten. After a fight he wasn't content to just win, he enjoyed reducing his opponent to a bloody senseless jelly. However, it was obvious to the other traders that his time as number one was nearing its end. And one day it arrived.

In tandem with the improving economic situation, the title King of the Market had evolved into an easy route to wealth. Many people had their sights set on defeating Big Hu. On the day of his downfall none of us knew that men in the employ of a Snakehead were on their way to town.

The term Snakehead is Chinese slang for the leader of a criminal gang. Many gangs were operating all over China. People in the West will recognise the word Snakehead in relation to the gangleaders who organise the annual migration of thousands of Chinese to the four corners of the world. The snakehead in this story wanted control of the market. The man on the motorcycle and two others in a stolen black van were there to see that he got it.

They arrived just after lunchtime and drew to a halt opposite Big Hu's shop. Only the van passenger entered. The other two remained with their vehicles. The passenger ordered and enjoyed a meal then refused to pay the bill and walked out. Big Hu, shouting angrily, chased after the man who, by now, was standing on the opposite pavement. Big Hu got halfway across the road before the van ran him down. As he instinctively rose to a kneeling position, the van reversed and ran over him again. When the van bounced over the body for the third time before driving away at speed, it was the head of Big Hu that took the weight, causing his skull to split wide open and the eyes to bulge out their sockets. He was instantly dead. The passenger cocked his leg over the pillion seat of the motorcycle and that too roared away.

In Market Street everyone stopped whatever they were doing and hurried to the roadside. What they saw was Big Hu lying in the road, the white mush of his brain mixing with the red blood running from his open head. Only after everyone had gathered and looked did someone think to report the incident to the police.

The van, made heavy by bags of sand, was found in the next village. No wonder it had crushed the skull of Big Hu. The criminals were never caught but to most people that wasn't too surprising. In those days people only had their suspicions; these days it is confirmed. Throughout China most police units were/are in the pay of snakeheads. It is also known that the local Communist Party Officials control the snakeheads.

After a reasonable period of doing almost nothing the police came to the conclusion that the death of Big Hu was an unfortunate accident. The body was released and duly arrived at the crematorium. It was in a terrible condition, giving the Mortician an almost impossible task to make Big Hu look acceptable to his family. He did his best but the eyes defeated him. Time and again he put them back into their sockets only to have them pop out again.

He asked La-la for advice. Said La-la, "As a boy my father taught me how to deal with pop-out eyes. Now I will show you."

He gently rubbed the right eye area with his thumb before making sure that the nerves and tissue were packed in such a way as to leave sufficient room for the ball. Carefully dropping the eyeball into the socket he cupped his left hand over the eye and smacked down hard with his right hand onto his left. When he removed his hands the eye was back in place.

La-la turned to the mortician and said, "Now you do the other." He did. Both eyes stayed in their sockets. However not even La-la could close the eyelids. Big Hu continued to glare angrily out at the world.

During the performance for Big Hu, his wife held her arms aloft and screamed her anguish. In addition to the many relatives, a large number of the townsfolk had crowded into the Memorial Hall where Big Hu's body lay in the glass coffin. Only his face was on show, eyes glowering. The eldest son, being the first to look into the coffin, had the presence of mind to cover the face with a silk square before allowing the rest to file past. Those attending wanted to hear La-la's on the road ballad, wondering what song he would compose for the bully.

> *The flowers glisten under the sun*
> *after spring rains have eased,*
> *while flowing waves of young rice*
> *pat banks of countless paddy fields.*
> *This is China, our Motherland*
> *where humans pass through in a trice,*
> *born to live by open hand, not fist.*

The congregation let go a collective sigh. Despite having just cause to do so, La-la was not going to sing a vindictive song. Most of the onlookers were disappointed. They had expected to hear La-la seek an appropriate punishment for Big Hu.

> *You stare upwards, high into the sky,*
> *are you searching for neutrality?*
> *That is not the way to go.*
> *Look down, you have to account for your cruelty.*
> *Your eyes will guide you to the Nether World*
> *tell Yama, the King of Hell, when you meet,*
> *that you will be good and kind, no insults hurled.*
> *La…la…la…la…la…la…la…la…*
> *Go peacefully on your road.*

Pandemonium!

The pro-La-la majority clapped and cheered, the rest booed or shouted. The loudest voice came from the widow. A big woman, she quickly sprang forward to grab a handful of La-la's hair with one hand and his jacket with the other while shouting, "How dare you curse my husband to Hell!" She was pulled away by several hands but still managed to pull out plenty of hair and two buttons off La-la's jacket.

By now the majority was chanting, "Yama is waiting to send Hu deep down!" Then fighting broke out. La-la was caught completely by surprise. Never before had one of his ballads caused such an uproar.

*

The funeral performance was a debating topic for many days. On the one hand the villagers criticised Widow Hu for her attack on La-la. On the other they expressed their disapproval of La-la's use of the unlucky word Hell. Eventually the episode was reported to Upstart, now the Governor of the County. We know that he was one of those unscrupulous politicians who use every opportunity to further their career, no matter who gets hurt. It had been him who had destroyed the cemeteries.

He decided that the Big Hu Incident, as it became known, was a good chance to get some favourable publicity for himself. He persuaded a tame journalist to write an article entitled Socialist Crematorium or Superstitious Rites? He then had the article printed on the front page of the local newspaper. The Communist Party controls all media.

The article attacked La-la, condemning his on the road ballads and accusing him of a systematic attempt to destroy the funeral reforms as approved by Beijing. The journalist proved his point by saying that La-la had used such unauthorised and unacceptable words as King of Hell therefore using a government-run establishment to advocate and promote religious superstition!

Unable to read, La-la went about his business completely unaware of his sudden loss of face until the Mortician read the article to him. To

La-la it was a worrisome puzzle. He had always composed his songs for the dead according to their circumstances and behaviour when alive. He had never before had any trouble and could not understand why his words were so wrong this time.

The Mortician hit the nail on the head when he replied, "Your life has always been with the dead. You have never learned to deal with the living. Everyone except you knows how hard the Governor has struggled to get himself noticed by Beijing. Now you have given him another opportunity."

The Director of the Crematorium was a worried man. In China there is always a scapegoat. It had been he who had recommended La-la's employment, making him fearful that the scandal was about to rebound onto him. He approached La-la in the courtyard of the crematorium and began to scold him loudly, knowing his public show of disapproval for La-la would be witnessed.

In the middle of his tirade a messenger from the County Town interrupted with the instruction that the Governor wanted to see the Director immediately.

La-la waited. Fearing the worst. Hoping for the best. When the Director returned during the early evening he went directly to La-la's room and knocked respectfully. When La-la opened the door and saw the look on the Director's face, he knew it was bad news.

"I'm sorry La-la. The Governor has given me his direct order. On the road ballads are banned and you must leave first thing in the morning."

This was La-la's most bitter blow. Not only had he lost his job, he could no longer sing his songs. He felt as if someone high above had hit him hard on the head with an invisible hammer.

The Director gave a sympathetic sigh. Beneath his thin veneer of political obedience a decent man was hiding. He knew how hard it was going to be for La-la and did his best to soften the blow. "You can take everything we issued to you and I will add an extra week to your severance pay. I wish I could do more but I can't, except to wish you well."

Then he did a most unusual thing. He held out his hand, western style, to shake hands with La-la. Hand-shaking had only recently arrived in China, brought by foreign business people. For the Director to offer his hand showed a very high degree of respect. La-la gladly took the offered hand in his and the men parted as friends.

*

It was a cold December morning when La-la left the crematorium. Grinding its gears, a noisy green pick-up truck carrying a cardboard coffin headed towards the gate. "Sorry Comrade," thought La-la bitterly. "No ballad to help you go down the road. Not for you. Not for anyone."

He didn't hurry. There was nothing in town for him except Cripple Li so it was afternoon when he knocked on his friend's door. No answer. He knocked again. No answer. Cripple Li was not at home. La-la decided to sit on the stairs and wait. As old men do, he nodded off.

It was dusk when La-la awoke to a shaking of his shoulder. "La-la, are you all right?" The open front door of a flat on the same landing allowed sufficient light for Cripple Li's neighbour to recognise La-la. Without waiting for an answer the neighbour continued to speak. "I'm so sorry about Cripple Li. He was a good neighbour. Never gave any trouble…"

La-la quickly interrupted, "What's happened? Is Cripple Li in trouble? Is he hurt?"

"Don't you know? He dropped dead in the street yesterday. Heart attack they said."

"Where is he?" cried La-la, struggling to his feet. "I have to go to him. He needs me to sing a down the road ballad."

"You're too late. They took him away to the crematorium this morning."

La-la remembered the pick-up and the cardboard coffin. Could it have been his old pal? If only he had composed a better ballad for Big Hu! The neighbour returned to his flat leaving La-la to deal with his grief alone. And alone he remained. Truly alone. No job, no home, no family and no friends.

*

From that day La-la was invisible to most people. Those who happened to notice saw a small wizened old man carrying a wicker basket on his arm, rummaging through rubbish. By eating thrown-away food and earning the few cents paid by the local recycling plant for bits of cloth, drinks cans, old bottles and newspapers - and by spending the cold winter nights in doorways, La-la survived.

December passed into January. People were getting ready to celebrate the most important Chinese holiday, the Spring Festival but to La-la it meant nothing. Staying alive for one more day was his only ambition.

When the ancients calculated that the Chinese New Year must begin at midnight of the first new moon following the passing of the old Lunar Year, they were living in the south of China where spring comes early. That's why they called it The Spring Festival. In our part of China it's still mid-winter. We have to wait for at least two more months for spring.

On the eve of the festival La-la was in Market Street rummaging as usual. He was as wrapped up against the severe cold as he could be, with an old towel wrapped around his neck and ears. As he chased an escaping wind-blown plastic bottle across the road, he didn't hear or see the official car approaching at speed. The car screeched to a halt but not before it had nudged La-la hard enough to make him fall.

The driver was completely unconcerned about whether La-la was hurt. Carrying a long line of firecrackers he climbed out of the car and lit the first cracker before throwing them over La-la. He watched, laughing loudly, as the firecrackers began to explode, one-by-one.

"That'll teach you to look before crossing a road." Shouted the driver.

A very frightened La-la, ears ringing from the explosions, passed out.

When his senses returned he was resting against a lamppost with the young Mortician holding a bottle of mineral water to his lips. Many people looked on but none offered help to this smelly old wreck. He was obviously an alcoholic or a drug addict.

The Mortician smiled and lifted La-la's head a little to allow the old man to drink. "You blocked the way of the Governor's car," he said. "He's got his promotion and was on his way to attend a farewell banquet before his departure for Beijing. Good riddance! I hope the snot-gobbling bastard dies of food poisoning. And his shit-faced driver is just as bad. He didn't care about causing an avalanche when he set off those firecrackers."

Feeling better, La-la looked around. The crowd began to drift away. He asked, "What are you doing here?"

"I came in to buy some things for the holiday and saw what happened. I couldn't believe it was you. How sad you look. Are you feeling better now?"

"Yes thank you." La-la struggled to his feet.

"I have to go," said the Mortician, as La-la drank the last of the water. "A flu' epidemic is killing off the sick and old. We are working double-shifts so that we can have a couple of days off. I'm working through the night and as usual I will be late for work but who cares?" He fished a few notes from his pocket and handed them to La-la. "That's all I have with me. Just enough for a hot meal and a warm drink. Good luck La-la. Happy holiday." He hurried away. La-la was alone again.

He sat under the plastic sheeting of a market stall. The traders had closed early on this special night. From all around him sounds of merriment and enjoyment attacked his ears, saddening him. The money had indeed bought a meal and hot tea, so he wasn't hungry. Just lonely. Never had he been so completely alone for a Spring Festival. He remembered times when he and his father had sung songs together, entertaining the villagers.

Last year he and Cripple Li had raised glasses of rice wine and wished each other good fortune. Huh! There had been no sign of good luck. Instead it had been the worst bad- luck year of his life.

"This horrible year is about to end and a new one will begin," he thought. "Then it will be my time." He had already made his New Year resolution.

From somewhere he could distinctly hear shouting and joyous squeals. The New Year had arrived. He crawled out from under the market stall and stood up. He knew he was weak in body but he felt spiritually lifted. For probably the first time in his entire life he was about to do something purely for himself. He raised his arms to the sky and turned round three times.

"A new century is here. I bid you welcome," he shouted. "Never before have I taken a day to use as I wish without having to worry about somebody else. This first day of the New Millennium is mine!" He headed for the crematorium.

CHAPTER 12

Little Rain

Life had been peaceful for the Woo family since their move to Yellow County but that ended when, in August 1986, a precious and unexpected gift arrived.

Shu Mei, irritable after a long and difficult working day, decided to walk the longer way home. She needed fresh air and time to regain her equilibrium.

What she got was a baby girl.

Her chosen route took her along the riverbank where she came across a dozen or so people staring down at a baby, wrapped in rags, lying in a hand-made willow basket. The baby was soundless and motionless, as if dead.

Always compassionate, Mei took the baby into her arms and opened the wrapping rags. A baby girl. A scrap of paper inside the rags bore her birth date. She was five days old. This is a common occurrence in China. Baby girls thrown away due to the one-child policy. Every household wants a boy. Only a boy can continue the family name and be the future breadwinner. A girl is a liability - a total loss. On her wedding day a girl moves to her in-laws, taking with her an acceptably large dowry. Anything less than acceptable causes an extreme loss of family face and disbarment from seeing the grandchild.

Each year the one-child policy signs the death warrant of tens of thousands of newborn girls plus thousands more girl foetuses being aborted.

Mei thought of her own daughter, Jasmine. Mei loved her so much. Never could she have abandoned her - not for anything. How could any mother do such a thing? For Mei it was an unanswerable question. For sure this baby *was* abandoned. Left to die. So what to do?

Mei gently replaced the wrappings and returned the child to the basket. It was not her concern. Best to let someone else do the caring. She had her own daughter to think about... It was then that she lost her own argument. As soon as Mei's hands left the tiny body, the baby began to cry - mewling weakly, plaintively. When Mei's hand returned to the body, the crying stopped.

"Ah! Look at that," said a woman. "She likes you. Fate has made you soul sisters. Take her home Comrade. She's yours now."

For sure Mei had felt an unexpected connection between herself and the child. Murmurs of agreement and nodding of heads. A man's voice said, "It is written."

*

When Woo Song saw the tiny girl-face, his first thought was to save her life. "She's beautiful," he said to Mei, "but she looks poorly. While you wash her, I'll go and buy some baby food, a bottle, teats, diapers and a blanket."

Disappointingly, when Mei offered the teat, the baby was too weak to suck, so they took her to the hospital.

"Her life is nearing its end," pronounced the Doctor. "She's weak from a lack of sustenance and she has pneumonia. We will do our best, but..." He shrugged his shoulders. "Please fill in this form and I will admit her."

Shu Mei and Woo Song were confronted with the first of the many problems that this tiny baby had brought with her.

Woo Song said to the doctor, "We can't tell you anything about her. She's a foundling. Abandoned on the riverbank. My wife couldn't leave her there to die."

The doctor sighed and looked out of the window. A gentle rain was falling. By rights he should not treat this child, but he was a compassionate man, true to his calling.

"She needs specialised hospital treatment," he said. "If you pay her medical bills nobody will care if she's yours or not. Complete the form as far as you can and I'll do the rest. For now, let's call her "Little Rain". If she survives, what happens to her will be your decision. Almost certainly, even after treatment, if you send her to the State Orphanage she will die."

Happily Little Rain did survive. Sadly, during her time in hospital, Woo Song's father, Woo Bao, died. To Woo Song and Shu Mei it could only be an omen. They must fill the void of Woo Bao's passing by raising Little Rain as their own. It was also what they wanted to do but first they had to consider the feelings of their real daughter.

Fortunately they needn't have worried. Jasmine immediately accepted Little Rain as her sister, so the matter was settled. For good or ill, Little Rain was a member of the Woo family.

*

Little Rain proved to be a bright, intelligent, bundle of delight. She began to smile at three months and at eight months said her first words, Mama, followed after a few days by Papa. Woo Song and Shu Mei were so happy, they truly believed that the Celestial Emperor had sent Little Rain to them. Any trouble that they might encounter along the way was more than compensated for by the pleasure of seeing her grow stronger and bigger.

The next, and most difficult problem, was the one-child policy. Within their jurisdiction, the local police were in charge of the registration of all births, deaths and marriages. Because Woo Song and Shu Mei already had a child properly and correctly registered, Little Rain could not have her own registration, nor could Woo Song adopt her. That was the law, said the Registration Officer.

The law also stated that an unregistered child could not attend school or university, or be given employment, or join the Communist Party.

What to do? They had heard rumours that bribery was the only way to get the Registration Officer to authorise a registration under an often-used reason of "exceptional circumstances".

They would try that.

*

Since about 1980, corruption has been a fact of life in China. From the lowest Communist Party Official to the highest level of Central Government, the higher up the political ladder the leaders are, the more money they extort. Almost every Party member is on the take. They prey on each other; openly steal State Allocated Funds and take every cent they can from the ordinary people.

In every city and town there are high street shops selling cheap cigarettes, tobacco, alcohol and other goods, but they don't get their supplies from the official wholesalers or manufacturers. Their stock comes from the Party Leaders, doctors, surgeons, nurses, schoolteachers, lowly clerks, policemen of all ranks... In fact, anyone with the smallest amount of authority over other people.

The goods openly sold in these particular shops are "gifts"... But they're not really gifts - they're bribes taken by those in authority to simply do their jobs properly or provide a service that a person is entitled to anyway. For example, in a hospital, everyone involved in an operation - the doctors, the theatre staff and the nurses, expect "gifts" of money or cigarettes or alcohol or goods from the patient (or the patient's family) merely to do a good job.

No "gifts" means no guarantee of a successful operation or good post-op nursing. In fact a patient without "gifts" will have a horrible time in hospital, and often will needlessly die. And, bear in mind, apart from the Party Members who are entitled to free medical services, the patients will have already paid high fees for the service.

All schools charge fees. In addition, parents are expected to give "gifts" to teachers and school staff. This ensures that their child will receive a good education, pass their exams, and graduate with good grades. No "gifts" equals no graduation diploma.

So the goods on sale in these particular shops are the "gifts" that are "surplus to requirement". For example, a doctor receiving a weekly supply of, (say), a dozen cartons of cigarettes, will keep what he wants for himself and send the rest to the special shop. The cut-price shop will sell the cigarettes to the public. The net profits will go back to the doctor.

It's illegal, but every Party Member supports the scheme, so the shop will never be raided by the police or closed down.

And this scheme is only the tip of the corruption iceberg!

*

Song and Mei talked long and hard. In their opinion, bright and intelligent Little Rain deserved to have an education. Therefore, they must pursue the possibility of registration.

They'd use their savings and if that didn't work, they would live most frugally on Song's salary and use Mei's wages to continue the struggle.

A large part of their savings went to buy the most expensive wine and cigarettes as gifts for the Leader and the Deputy Leader of the local police. Yes, the presents were safely delivered. No, they were not returned, nor were they acknowledged.

Throughout the next few years, Song and Mei spent the rest of their savings and all of Mei's wages regularly wining and dining the leading government officials of Yellow County. Oh yes, the officials gobbled up the food, guzzled the alcohol and had a high old time at Song and Mei's expense, but none helped Little Rain get her registration.

Also, during those years, Little Rain had health problems. Born sickly, so she remained - needing medical treatment that had to be paid for, yet Song and Mei steadfastly refused to give up on her. Every available cent was spent on Little Rain, with nothing except the bare essentials spent on Song, Mei and Jasmine, yet, remarkably, the four of them remained a tight, loving, happy family unit.

By now Little Rain was almost six years old - school age. Beautiful, bright and as sharp as a tack, she was still a member of the "Black Society". That was the nickname given to all Chinese people not having been registered and, by 1992, there were millions and millions of them!

Many women, especially those living in the remote regions of China, secretly give birth to more than one child. And all of those "extra" children automatically become members of the Black Society - their very existence considered to be illegal by Central Government.

Officially, the Black Society does not exist.

*

The school year was divided into two terms. Mid February to early July was one term. The first day of September to mid January was the other. Song and Mei badly wanted Little Rain to attend the local school but, as a member of the Black Society, she had no right to receive any sort of education. Only money could make it possible. The going rate at this school for each "legal" child was 500yuan per term, plus gifts. For an "illegal", the cost was the normal tuition fee of 500yuan plus a "donation" of 5000yuan per term to enable the teachers to organise "extra-curricular activities" plus gifts. In fact no extra-curricular activities ever took place, just normal homework.

That was the situation, take it or leave it. Sadly Song and Mei had no choice but to leave it.

*

"Comrade Woo Song!"

The call came from behind him. Song turned and with a huge smile on his face he exclaimed, "What a wonderful surprise. I didn't recognise you in your new clothes." He offered his hand in friendship as he continued, "How are you?"

Guang Da and son, Guang Guang, bowed respectfully before shaking the outstretched hand. They too were smiling. "Actually," said Guang Da, nodding towards a teahouse, "we were looking for you Comrade Song. Please, take tea with us... We need to have discussions with you."

Guang Da steered Woo Song to a corner table and the three men sat down. Nothing special was discussed until the tea had been served, then Guang Da leaned forward and in a low voice said, "Comrade Woo Song, my son and I have never forgotten your kindness to us at the railway station. If you hadn't helped us that day, we probably wouldn't have got home. Also, your esteemed father, Comrade Stationmaster Woo Bao, and yourself, were responsible for my son and I being given the title of People's Servants. It is a debt that we cannot ever repay, and I know that you would never wish it to be repaid. That is your way. That was also your Father's way. However, my son and I have been thinking that perhaps we can return just a small part of our indebtedness to you."

Song, in total surprise, sat back in his seat and blinked several times before mumbling, "It was a small thing. Nothing, nothing at all."

"Oh yes, Comrade Song, it was something... A big something. During the last seven years my son and I have learned much. Yours and your esteemed father's acts of kindness were a rarity in a world full of greed and selfishness. Modern life is all about 'take, take, take', with almost no 'give' at all..."

"Please Comrade Guang Da,' interrupted Song. "It isn't worth a mention. You and Guang Guang have proved to be worthy of your positions as People's Servants, and your works of art are wonderful. That is more than sufficient repayment. "

Guang Da thought for a few seconds, wondering exactly how best to broach the real reason for this talk. Chinese custom and etiquette demanded a "round the houses" approach, but Guang Da was a peasant, and peasants, with so much work to do, had little time for such niceties.

"There's another person that we can help." Said Guang Da.

"There is?"

"Yes. Little Rain."

"Pardon? Are you referring to *my* Little Rain?"

"Yes. We hear a lot of gossip in our line of work. Many of the bereaved people who come to us to order a plaque have a need to talk, and your name is often mentioned. Almost everybody, even the policemen, applauds your decision to raise Little Rain as your own."

"They do?"

"Yes, and they know about your attempts to get her registered, *and* the huge school fees, *and* the medical bills, *and* how you are struggling to pay everything, *and* the sacrifices of your family."

Song bristled with anger. "What business is it of theirs? I...."

"Comrade Woo Song. Please don't be angry." Interrupted Guang Da. "Although our few huts have grown into a town, it's still a village at heart, with gossip being our newspaper. And anyway, most of the people support you and your sacrifices. They think you and Shu Mei are wonderful. So do we - that is why we are having this discussion. We want to help Little Rain go to school."

Guang Da and Guang Guang, with their government salaries plus a healthy income from private work, could easily afford the tuition fees and the twice-yearly donations, so Little Rain, at age six, went to school.

She did not disappoint. She studied hard, was well behaved and got on with other students. At the end of her first year, and every year after that, she was made class leader. At age twelve, despite her frequent visits to the hospital, she graduated with honours from Primary School.

And that was where the problems of registration again caused trouble. It was now 1997. Greed and corruption was out of control. For Little Rain to enter Junior Middle School, the Headmaster demanded 1500yuan for tuition and a donation of 15,000yuan per term. Meanwhile Guang Da had died and Guang Guang was recently married and despite Woo Song teaching Guang Guang to read and write, his wife decided that the school payments for Little Rain must stop. Although she wasn't pregnant, the money must be put by to educate *her* child, not wasted on "that sickly illegal foundling".

Woo Song and Shu Mei were at their wits end. What to do now?

It was Woo Song's mother who, more in jest than as a serious suggestion, came up with the only viable idea. "If you two got divorced, Jasmine would automatically belong to her mother. That's the law. And if Shu Mei took Jasmine away to live somewhere else, Song would no longer have a child. He could then legally adopt Little Rain and register her as his daughter."

On hearing this, Mei burst into tears. She knew it was a good idea. She also knew it was the only idea that would work, but to deliberately destroy the family… It broke her heart just to think about it.

Mei and Song had known each other since babyhood. They'd lain on the same baby blanket in the shade of the same courtyard tree, toddled in the same dust, shared their toys, walked to school hand-in-hand, fallen in love. Their young love maturing and merging into a single entity. How could one survive without the other?

For many days Mei refused to discuss it, whilst all the while thinking how to satisfy both things - Little Rain legally registered *and* keeping the family intact. She was stuck in a quandary, unable to advance or retreat, constantly leaning one way and then the other.

In the end she concluded that there had only ever been one choice - support Little Rain.

*

The official reason for the divorce was simple; they were no longer in love. Mei and Song handed their applications to the leaders of their individual work units requesting their permission to divorce. Without the approval of both work unit leaders, their divorce would not be legitimised by the registration office leader. Naturally three envelopes stuffed with cash was also needed. One to each leader.

As is usual in these cases, from the moment that the divorce applications were granted, the malicious gossip began. Divorce was still frowned upon, so the couple was fair game. "It's all Woo Song's doing. He has a secret lover," said one. "Shu Mei has discovered that Little Rain is Woo Song's love child," said another.

A third said, "No, no, no. Shu Mei is the one with a lover. Why else would she have suddenly brought Little Rain to her home?"

The gossip was ignored. Most people guessed why the couple had divorced and were either extraordinarily sympathetic or keeping their noses out of it.

The members of the Neighbourhood Committee didn't care one way or the other provided they had an opportunity to throw their weight around. Since 1949, when the Communists took power in China, the most detested of all of the Party organisations have been the Neighbourhood Committees. Made up from retired Communist Party members plus a few junior Party Officials making their way up the political ladder, these busybodies have patrolled their neighbourhoods poking their noses into everybody's business and reporting anything suspicious.

It is illegal for a divorced couple to live in the same building. On the day of the divorce, the Neighbourhood Committee ordered Shu Mei and Jasmine out of the family home, giving them no time to say a proper goodbye to Song or Little Rain.

That was the end of the marriage.

*

Woo Song lost no time in submitting his request to legally adopt Little Rain. The Party Official in charge of adoption made Woo Song write a personal guarantee saying he would never remarry. The official notary certified the document after witnessing Woo Song place his inked right-hand index finger on the paper. Two more money-stuffed envelopes changed hands and the deed was done. At last Little Rain was legally registered as Woo Song's daughter.

Woo Song and Shu Mei dared not meet each other. For sure the Neighbourhood Committee would have reported them. Li Lan was their secret go-between, passing news to and fro and delivering letters of love.

Then, during the school summer holiday of 1999, Little Rain again fell ill.

This time it was serious... Very expensively serious. The doctor said that Little Rain's first five days of life when she had been neglected by her birth-mother, and the subsequent attack of pneumonia, had left a severe weakness that needed a heart-and-lung transplant. The hospital could keep Little Rain alive for a while but if a suitable match wasn't found...

Money had always been a problem, and lots of money was now needed to pay for the treatment and the transplant. It was no good approaching Guang Guang. There was no sympathy in the heart of his wife. This was the way of it in modern-day China.

Li Lan arranged a secret meeting in the tea-room of a hotel - one of many new hotels being built all over China. "It's time for the family to reunite," she said. "It was broken for Little Rain's sake and now you must get together again for her sake. The savings made by only having one household would enable Little Rain to get the treatment she needs."

"We can't. I gave my sworn guarantee to stay single." Said Woo Song. "If I break it, I'll go to prison."

"No you won't," replied Li Lan. "The Party Official who handled the adoption of Little Rain has moved on. His replacement is new to the town. If you keep quiet about Little Rain, what's to stop you remarrying?"

Eight days later the divorce ended.

*

Little Rain was dying. The whole family, including Jasmine and Li Lan, took turns to sit beside her bed by day and by night. The doctors said the brave little girl was a fighter, but even her magnificent spirit could not save her. Only a transplant could have done that but sadly, no suitable donor had been found.

On Chinese New Year's Eve, the doctors warned the gathered family that the end was near, and at exactly midnight, sweet, beautiful brave Little Rain passed away knowing that Woo Song, Shu Mei and Jasmine had made her the happiest, most-loved girl. A gift given to them by the Celestial Emperor.

Woo Song was the first to stop weeping and stand up. "I must get La-La to sing for her, otherwise she will never return to the Celestial Emperor."

Such was the power that had been attached to La-La. He was never to know that the people believed him to be a mythical creature sent from heaven to ensure a safe passage for the dead. If La-la wasn't at the funeral, the dead couldn't join their ancestors.

But it was too late. La-la was walking through heavy snow towards his own death.

*

Snow began to fall and the nearer La-la got to his destination the larger the flakes. Everywhere was white, including him. The guard on duty at the crematorium gate was huddled in his hut trying to keep warm. He didn't notice the white figure glide silently into the compound. The only clues to prove that someone had walked in were footprints quickly disappearing under new snow.

La-la went straight to the Memorial Hall and let himself in. It was bitterly cold. Indeed, probably because it was no longer being used it seemed to be colder inside than out. La-la removed his outer clothing, his gloves, his headgear and his black funeral-singer boots before climbing into the empty glass coffin. Goodness it was cold! He pulled on the new shoes given to him by Widow Yi. He wanted spotless shoes when he met his ancestors. Very solemnly and peacefully he lay down and settled himself.

For a short while he felt quite comfortable until the icy cold began to gnaw at his extremities. Soon he was shivering all over his body and his teeth chattered but he was determined to stay put. This was his time, his decision, his funeral. No politician or Communist busybody was going to spoil it.

He closed his eyes and waited until the cold had sufficiently penetrated his muscles and his blood. He felt as if he was floating. It was time. He opened his mouth and in a quiet, gentle voice began to sing his own carefully composed on the road ballad...

On the road I walk
now that I am old.
I have lived my life
serving the people
with my heart and soul.
I need not cry, nor need I smile,
there is nothing left for me
on this side of life.

This resting-place is my rickshaw
taking me to Nether Land.
See, my road is wide.
My love for the world
has been profound,
I helped the lost be found.
Now I fly from this world to the next,
to see Yama underground.

Uncounted souls I helped their road to see,
with countless songs I composed.
I see ancestral spirits greeting me
as I sing myself down the road.
This is my time. I choose to go.

Go well La-la, go well,
I float away like a tiny cloud.
La...la...la...la............

His voice faded away as he expelled his last contented breath.

*

That's not quite the end of my story. Later that year during the heavy monsoon rains a landslide happened high in the mountain nearest to the crematorium. Such occurrences are commonplace and as there were no casualties the event passed without notice.

However, not long afterwards a little boy attending a funeral pointed and said, "Look, there's La-la and Cripple li!" And indeed it seemed so. The landslip had left two rock columns standing side by side, silhouetted against the sky. One column was wide and squat. The other was a little shorter and leaned to one side.

Suddenly the mother of the deceased said she could hear a distant voice. "Listen, can you hear it under the wind?" Others then said they could.

Since then, many thousands of mourners have passed that way and most make a small nod of their head towards the faraway rocks. Political oppression means they cannot openly kow-tow for fear of arrest by the Communists, so they nod a respectful greeting. Mourners without number have claimed the honour of hearing the distant voice sing a down the road ballad for the recently departed.

La-la and Cripple Li live on in legend and once again superstition has defeated political oppression.

I suppose it always will.

*

Oh yes, there's one more thing...

Remember Ying Jun - also known as Threelips? Well, he did very well. His boiled chicken business flourished, allowing him to open more shops. Then he purchased his first American fried chicken franchise, then another, and another, and so on, and on, so that now, in April 2009, he's a very rich man.

My name is Mei-Li, meaning Little Beauty. I'm fifteen years old and I am the daughter of Ying Jun.

When I was aged twelve my father purchased what had once been Big King's house. He said the air was healthier than the polluted cities. He was extremely upset when he heard what had happened to La-la. It was then that he told me his life story. Of how he had been found as a child by a very kind man named La-la, and what happened between them.

He deeply regretted his bad behaviour and was saddened to realise that I would never know my grandfather... The wonderful man known as La-la. So I decided to find out more about him, and from that, has come this story.

I hope I have done him justice.

I exist. Therefore La-la's life was not wasted.

Sincerely,

La-la's loving and deeply respectful granddaughter,

Mei-Li.

*

THE FUNERAL SINGER

A fanciful fusion of fact, fiction and folklore.